Midnight on Lundy

By Victoria Eveleigh

Illustrated by Chris Eveleigh

Many people have helped me
gather information for this story.
I am especially grateful to Diana Keast, Chris Price,
Peggy Garvey, Jan Symons, Penny and Kate Ogilvie, Bridget Long,
Mary Courtenay, Mary Oldham, David Dyke, Lars Liwendahl,
and Mary Gade and her daughters, Jane and Anne-Marie,
for making my research so fascinating and enjoyable.
I would also like to thank the good friends who gave me helpful
feedback about the story.

This story is fictitious, as are all the people in it.

ISBN 978-0-9542021-3-2

Printed in Great Britain by Short Run Press Ltd
Book design by Sally Chapman-Walker

Published and distributed by
Tortoise Publishing
sales@tortoise-publishing.co.uk
www.tortoise-publishing.co.uk
Tel: (01598) 752310

For Diana,
with thanks

This story is set in the 1960s, when Lundy was still in private ownership. There were lighthouse-keepers in the North and South Lights, and the island was home to a close-knit community of resourceful, hard-working people who were often great characters.
Everyone who remembers that time says what fun it was.
I have tried to reflect the spirit of that period in Lundy's history while keeping all the characters, including the owners, completely fictional.

All the places on Lundy in the story are real, because it's difficult to create imaginary places on such a well-known island. However, several locations on the mainland are fictional, including St Anne's School, Home Farm, Highridge Farm and Rockleigh Manor.

Livestock no longer have to swim out to a boat off the Landing Beach to be transported to the mainland. In fact, ponies can now make the entire journey in a horsebox, thanks to the new jetty which was completed in 2000.

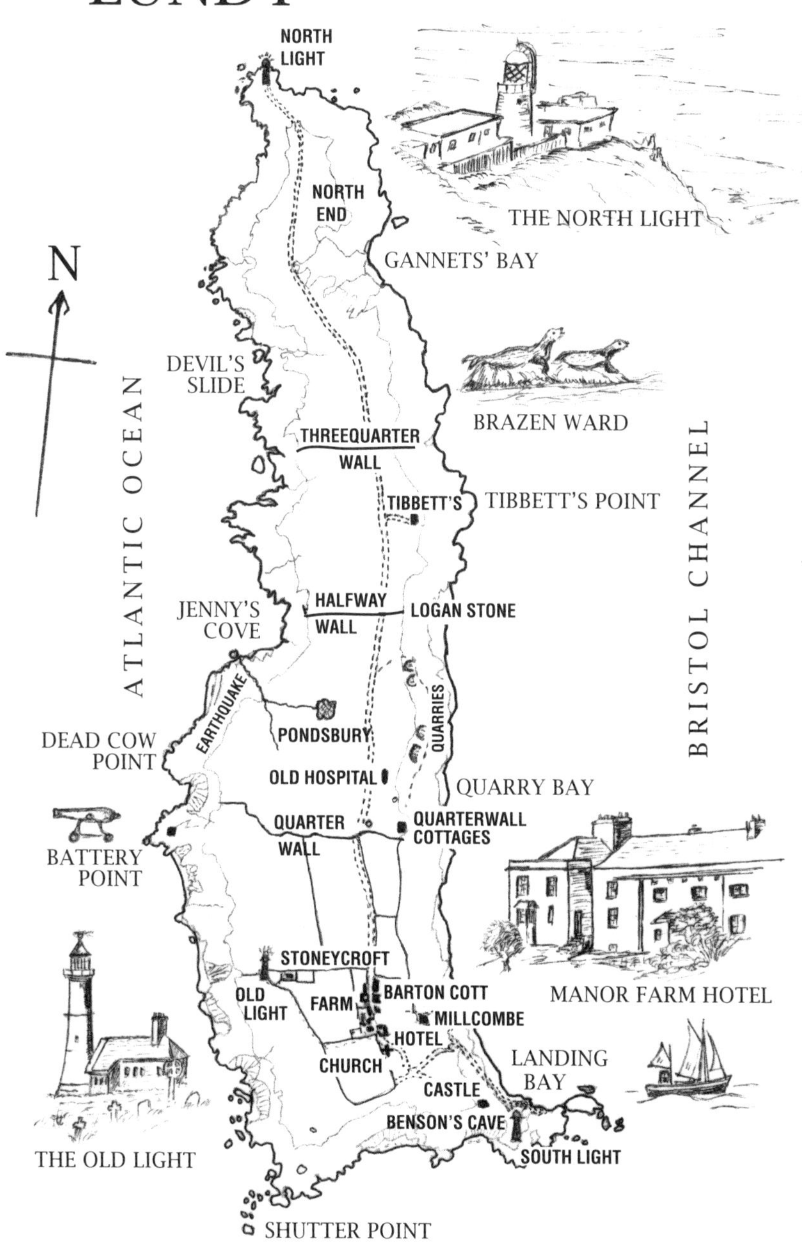
LUNDY
NORTH LIGHT
THE NORTH LIGHT
NORTH END
GANNETS' BAY
N
DEVIL'S SLIDE
BRAZEN WARD
ATLANTIC OCEAN
BRISTOL CHANNEL
THREEQUARTER WALL
TIBBETT'S
TIBBETT'S POINT
HALFWAY WALL
LOGAN STONE
JENNY'S COVE
EARTHQUAKE
QUARRIES
PONDSBURY
DEAD COW POINT
OLD HOSPITAL
QUARRY BAY
QUARTER WALL
QUARTERWALL COTTAGES
BATTERY POINT
STONEYCROFT
OLD LIGHT
FARM
BARTON COTT
MANOR FARM HOTEL
MILLCOMBE
HOTEL
CHURCH
LANDING BAY
CASTLE
BENSON'S CAVE
SOUTH LIGHT
THE OLD LIGHT
SHUTTER POINT

Chapter One

Jenny fled up the stony track from the village. "I won't go! *I won't!*" she shouted.

The wind snatched her words and carried them away over the sea towards the mainland – towards that other world which had played little part in her life, until now.

I'm perfectly happy living with Dad, she said to herself, and I've got plenty of friends. There are the islanders, lighthouse-keepers, fishermen, summer workers, visitors; you can't have many more friends than that! So why does Dad think I need to make friends and learn about the world? Why will it be *good* for me to go away to that stupid school?

"*Stupid, stupid school!*" Jenny screamed into the screaming wind.

She struggled to shut the gate at Quarter Wall. Then she turned and ran, with the wind chasing her, towards the quarries.

What if nobody likes me? she worried. What if I don't like them? It'll be like going to prison. Miles from Lundy, miles from Dad and, worst of all, miles from Midnight.

Jenny couldn't remember life without Midnight. He'd been the herd stallion since before she was born. He was the king, and Lundy was his kingdom. He roamed where he liked, jumping the walls with ease, and he took orders from nobody. Everyone who had tried to catch and tame him had failed miserably.

Everyone except Jenny – but that was their secret.

Jenny picked her way down the slippery path to the old quarries, knowing where she'd choose to shelter from a south-westerly gale if she were a pony.

She was right. The ponies were in the second quarry, protected from the elements by its massive walls, which made a kind of open cave looking out to sea. It was a peaceful sanctuary, while the storm raged all around and waves crashed against the rocks below.

Three foals had been born so far. Jenny sat down on a slab of granite, and watched as they played together. She loved their ruffled, fluffy baby coats. Two foals were a creamy colour with pale grey legs. They'd probably end up golden dun with black points, like Midnight. The third foal was a light roan. Foals had to be the best baby animals in the world.

The mares dozed, or wandered around picking at the plants that grew between the stones. They took no notice of the small, slender girl in their midst.

Jenny had spent so much time with the ponies that they probably thought she was another feral animal – once domesticated, but now gone wild, like them. She liked the idea. Mrs Hamilton was always calling her a wild child.

"Why, oh *why?*" Jenny cried out, startling a couple of mares nearby. "Oops, sorry!" she said, lowering her voice. "I mean, why does anything have to change? Why can't Mrs Hamilton carry on teaching me? She must have done a pretty good job so far, or I wouldn't have got that scholarship, would I? And why was I told that exam was just a test to see how well I was doing?"

She gazed at the idyllic scene before her, and sighed. "I

can't go away! I *can't!*" she said.

As if in agreement, Midnight walked up and nuzzled her short brown hair.

Jenny looked into his extraordinary midnight-blue eyes. "I wish I were a pony, Midnight. Life's simple for you, isn't it? You don't have to worry about exams and schools, or being sent to the mainland. All you have to do is find water, food and shelter."

Midnight gave a snort.

Jenny's cold fingers snuggled into the warm, soft hair under his thick mane. "Okay, so you have to take care of the mares and foals, I suppose, but that's not a hard job, is it? They pretty well take care of themselves, leaving you plenty of time to do as you please." She stood up on the granite slab and leant over Midnight's broad back.

He shifted his weight slightly, but didn't move away.

Without a second thought, Jenny leapt lightly onto him, and sat there as if it were the most natural thing in the world. It didn't even occur to her that riding a wild stallion without a saddle or bridle was dangerous.

He wandered along the old quarry terrace, in search of better grazing, and then browsed his way back to the mares again. Jenny just sat there and talked about anything and everything.

Midnight and Jenny seemed to have an understanding; he allowed her to sit on his back, and she let him do as he pleased – mainly because she didn't know how to get him to do anything else.

"I wish I could ride properly," Jenny told him. "Then we could gallop over the island, jumping everything in our way. Wouldn't that be fun?"

Riding lessons were the one thing Jenny longed for which she couldn't get on Lundy. Nobody else on the island seemed particularly interested in the ponies, beyond the fact they were nice to look at and had become a traditional part of Lundy – almost as popular as puffins with the tourists.

If only Mum...Jenny began to think, and then stopped herself. Dad said 'if onlys' could drive you mad, and he was right.

By the time they got back to the quarry, Jenny's brown corduroy trousers were cold and clammy from Midnight's damp back. They clung uncomfortably, chilling her body to shivering point.

"Time to go home and face the music," she said, giving Midnight a farewell rub on his shoulder.

His lips quivered in ecstasy, and his eyes started to close.

"You big baby!" she teased. "It's lucky nobody else knows what a softie you are. Promise me you'll stay wild with everyone else, won't you? You'll stay safe and free if you're wild."

Midnight nudged Jenny with his nose.

"Good boy," she said, scratching him under his chin. "Now, I really must be going."

Although Jenny was cold, she ambled home reluctantly, taking the longer route through the north entrance to the quarries. The wind had calmed to a fresh breeze, and a watery sun, like a torch with flat batteries, hung low over Pondsbury. She hadn't realised how late it was.

As she walked past the farm buildings she saw her father, Robert Medway, walking towards her with his long, easy stride. There was no escape; she'd have to talk to him.

"I've fed your animals for you," he said, without any sign of resentment. "Do you want to help me with the chickens?"

Why was he acting as if nothing had happened? A few

hours ago she'd screamed all sorts of hateful things at him. She scuffed some gravel with her foot. "Okay."

"I'll get the corn, and you can collect the eggs," he said.

Jenny never tired of egg-collecting; it was like hunting for treasure. She went to the back of the wooden chicken shed, and opened the flap covering the nesting boxes.

The rusty hinges creaked.

She felt inside, her fingers searching for smooth eggs nestling in the straw. Instead, they dipped into the slimy contents of a jagged eggshell. As she withdrew her fingers something furry writhed against them. She snatched her hand away and peered cautiously into the long, dark box.

A large rat glared back, whiskers twitching, surrounded by a gooey mess of broken eggshells. It leapt out of the box, and ran for cover under the shed.

Jenny screamed and jumped back, dropping the flap with a bang.

Robert hurried over, corn spilling from the feed scoop in his hand. "What's happened? Are you all right?"

"A rat! A really big one! Under there!" she squeaked. "All the eggs are broken! Ruined!"

Robert swore. "They've been in the vegetable garden, too; it's a never-ending battle. Poor old you!" He hugged his daughter, holding her close.

Jenny loved his hugs. They were safe and solid - a port in a storm.

"Ah well, rabbit stew for supper tonight," Robert said.

All the tensions of the day welled up and exploded inside Jenny, like a wave crashing to shore. She burst into tears.

"Hey, what's up?"

"Everything! I hate rats and I hate rabbit stew!" she wailed into her father's coat.

He stroked her damp hair. "I bet they don't eat rabbit stew at St Anne's."

Oh no! Jenny thought, here comes the lecture.

Robert hugged her tightly, engulfing her thin body in his strong arms. "I'm so proud of you," he said. "A scholarship to St Anne's really is a great achievement, you know."

"But I don't want to go, Dad! I know I'll hate it there!" She glanced up at him. "And why didn't you tell me it was a scholarship exam? Why did you lie?"

"Oh, Jenny! I thought you'd love to go away to school and be with children your own age for a change, rather than being stuck here with me the whole time. I couldn't afford to send you without the money for the scholarship, but I didn't want you to feel under pressure, or to be disappointed if you failed. It was a white lie, I suppose."

"What's a white lie?"

"A lie told to avoid hurting someone's feelings."

"Oh. Well, it didn't work, did it?" Jenny looked up again, and met her father's concerned gaze. "This is my home. I love it here. Why does anything have to change? Please don't make me go!"

"Of course I won't *make* you go Jenny, but you'll be missing the greatest opportunity of your life, and a lot of fun, too." Robert lowered his voice to a secret whisper. "I've heard there are stables nearby, and riding's an optional extra. You'd be able to have lessons every week. Would you like that?"

Riding lessons! Jenny thought. Perhaps if she went to school for a little while – just a term or two – she could learn to ride and then come home again for good. Riding lessons cost a lot of money, though. And she'd need riding clothes, like the girls in the *Princess Pony Annual* Mrs Hamilton had given her for Christmas. It would all be hopelessly expensive.

"Would you like riding lessons?" Robert asked again.

"Of course I would, but we can't afford it," she answered. "Also, I'd need boots, a hat, jodhpurs, a jacket and a yellow polo neck." She'd always longed for a yellow polo neck. She imagined herself looking like the girl on the front cover of the annual.

"I expect we'll manage somehow. Summer's coming up, so you'll be able to earn some money in the Hotel, and I'll get all the extra jobs I can. If you want riding lessons, you shall have them."

Jenny couldn't help smiling now. "Do you mean it?"

Robert smiled back. "Of course I mean it."

"I suppose school *could* be okay, if there's riding as well."

"I bet it'll be more than okay. It'll be great fun, you wait and see." Robert put his arm round Jenny's shoulder and turned towards home. "Meg! That'll do!" he called to his sheepdog as she tried, in vain, to get at the rat under the chicken shed.

A new world of possibilities opened up to Jenny. "Perhaps I could keep my own pony at the stables," she said, secretly thinking of Midnight.

Robert laughed and ruffled her hair. "Don't push your luck, young lady!"

Ah well, it was worth a try.

CHAPTER TWO

Typical, Jenny thought as she made sandwiches in the Hotel kitchen. It's the first day which really feels like summer, and it's a boat day. Still, the boat leaves at four-thirty, so there'll be time for a swim before I go to see the ponies.

On boat days hundreds of visitors came by steamer to visit Lundy, and they all had to be fed and looked after. Boat days were hard work for everyone, but they brought much-needed money to the island.

Jenny spread butter on slices of bread, put in the fillings, cut the sandwiches and stacked them on a tray. Her hands made sandwiches, but her mind thought ponies. Kittiwake, the youngest mare, would be having her first foal soon. Kit was quite tame, probably because she'd known Jenny since she was a foal. She was beautiful, with four white socks and a white star, and her body was a mottled grey-brown colour, like Lundy granite. Her foal was bound to be...

"There you are, Jenny!" Mrs Hamilton stood at the kitchen door. "There's someone I want you to meet. She's your age, and she's pony-mad, like you! You'd love to spend some time with her and show her the sights, wouldn't you? Don't worry about helping me in the Tea Garden this afternoon, I'll manage."

"Um..."

"Splendid! Here we are, then. Isabella, this is Jenny Medway, our farm manager's daughter. Jenny, this is Isabella Wagstaff."

Jenny was sure Mrs Hamilton had got Isabella's age wrong; she looked at least sixteen, rather than twelve. To Mrs Hamilton, 'a girl of your own age' could mean anyone from six to sixteen.

Isabella wore navy blue deck shoes with white laces, skimpy navy blue shorts and a matching blue striped T-shirt. Her arms and legs were long, slim and sun-tanned, and her silky dark hair was tied back with a navy blue ribbon.

Usually Jenny didn't care what she looked like, but at that moment she felt terribly small and self-conscious in her baggy hand-me-down khaki shorts and faded yellow Aertex shirt.

"Well, I can see you two are going to get along famously, so I'll leave you to your adventures!" said Mrs Hamilton. "I must get on. Remember, the boat leaves at four-thirty. Have fun!" The click-clack of her shoes faded as she marched away down the corridor.

Isabella and Jenny stood staring at each other, as if they were from different planets.

Sheila, the cook, broke the silence. "You get going, Jenny. I'll finish up here. Take a couple of sandwiches, if you like."

Sheila was short, plump, Scottish and, Jenny guessed, about thirty. She had curly red hair and the sort of freckled skin which never tanned, even in mid-summer. Mr Hamilton called her 'a good sort'. Jenny guessed that meant she was a hard worker, totally dependable and rather dull.

"Thanks, Sheila. Is a cheese sandwich OK for you, um,

Isabella?" asked Jenny.

"Fine," said Isabella, without enthusiasm.

Usually Jenny enjoyed showing visitors the island, but she felt like a fish out of water with Isabella. Still, taking her sightseeing had to be better than making sandwiches.

"Where would you like to go?" she asked, as they walked out into the bright sunshine.

"I don't know. You're the guide," Isabella replied.

"Okay. How about starting with the Church, as we're so close to it?"

"Why has such a small place got such a huge church? Are you all very religious or something?"

"Not especially, but the person who built it was. He was a vicar, and he owned Lundy in Victorian times," Jenny explained. "Do you want to look inside?"

Isabella sighed. "If we *must*. Isn't there anything more exciting to do?"

"Um, how about the Castle? It's not far, and there's a lovely view from there. We'll be able to see the steamer in the Landing Bay."

Jenny tried to make conversation by telling Isabella about places of interest along the way, but she didn't seem at all interested. They lapsed into an awkward silence.

As they reached the Castle, Isabella said, "Doesn't look much like a castle to me. More like a badly built house with no windows."

"It's the oldest building on Lundy. It's got tons of history," Jenny said, ready with tales of the Mariscos, Thomas Benson and dastardly deeds.

"I'll take your word for it," Isabella replied.

"Let's go down to Benson's Cave. There's a great view from there." Jenny led the way down the steep bank to the cave.

Isabella slipped on the grass in her deck shoes, and ended up inching down cautiously on her bottom, glancing nervously at the sheer drop to her right. "This had better be worth it," she said, dusting herself off. She peered in through the narrow entrance to Benson's Cave, and wrinkled her nose. "Is this little hole supposed to be a cave?"

"I know it doesn't look much, but it's quite large inside. It was used for storing smuggled goods," Jenny said.

"Wow-ee!" Isabella mocked.

When all else fails, eat, Jenny thought, sitting down on a grassy ledge near the cave. She handed a couple of sandwiches to Isabella, who took them without a word of thanks.

After nibbling a bit from the centre, Isabella threw most of her sandwich over the cliff. Before long a couple of gulls found the easy meal. Then others swooped in. Soon a riot of gulls squabbled beneath them. Fascinated, Isabella tore up her second sandwich and tossed it down to them, bit by bit.

Jenny was shocked. Food was never wasted or taken for granted on Lundy.

While Isabella fed the gulls, Jenny ate her sandwiches. The sun shone from a cloudless sky, picking out every detail of the breathtaking scenery around them. Boats of various sizes speckled the bright blue sea, and clustered round the steamer in the bay to the left. Ahead, the rocky peninsula of Lametor rose up like a monster from the deep, topped by the gleaming white bulk of the South Light.

This must be the most beautiful place on earth, Jenny thought.

"I pity the poor person who has to live there," said Isabella, pointing at the lighthouse.

"Albert lives there – Albert Scoines. He's the PK. He says

it's the best job in the world."

"What on earth's a PK?"

"Principal Keeper. You see, the lighthouses on Lundy are rock lights, so there are three resident keepers in each. The keepers live there together, while their families live on the mainland. They do two months on duty, and then have a month's leave ashore. The PK is the head man in each light."

"Fascinating," Isabella murmured. She was lying on the grass with her eyes closed.

Jenny wasn't good at spotting sarcasm. "The PK of the North Light is Gareth. He's okay, but he sometimes gets a bit moody after a few beers. Albert is definitely the nicest keeper. In fact, he's the nicest person I know – apart from Dad, of course."

Isabella's eyes remained closed. "What about your mother?"

Jenny froze. All the islanders knew what had happened to Mum, so she'd never had to tell anyone before. It wasn't that Mum was never mentioned; islanders and regular visitors alike often spoke fondly of her, and in the Tavern there was a lovely picture of her sitting on her beloved Lundy pony, Puffin, with Jenny's Cove in the background. She'd lived on Lundy for eight years, working on the farm, looking after the ponies and carrying out bird surveys for the Field Society. Everyone had liked Jane Medway.

The gulls stopped squawking. The cliffs fell silent, as if holding their breath, willing Jenny to reply.

"She died when I was five." There, she'd said it.

Isabella looked embarrassed. She sat up and picked at the grass by her side. Then she said brightly, "Oh well, mothers are pretty useless, really. Daddy always says Mummy's main function in life is to spend money as fast as he can make it."

Jenny stared at her, speechless. There was a long, uncomfortable silence.

Isabella looked down again, and picked away at the grass. “I love going abroad, don’t you?” she said. “Properly abroad, I mean, like the Mediterranean.”

Jenny gave up trying to be polite. “Why did you come here, then?”

With a disarming smile, Isabella said, “Daddy’s come here on some sort of business, so I thought it would be rather fun to come, too. He’s got an important meeting with the owner, Mr Bonham, and someone called, er, Donald Hamilton?”

“Mr Hamilton’s the agent. He lives here.”

"Oh, I see. That would explain why Daddy's meeting him. Anyway, this is just a day trip. We're all going to America for a proper family holiday in August. Where do you go for your summer holidays?"

Before she could stop herself Jenny said, "Corfu." It was the first place which sprang to mind because she'd been reading *My Family and Other Animals* by Gerald Durrell. Albert had given it to her.

"Really? Isn't Corfu great? We went there last year!" Isabella exclaimed. "Did you go to the Canal D'Amour?"

"Oh yes, we went all over the place," Jenny replied. What on earth was she playing at? An occasional trip to Bideford or Ilfracombe was her idea of going abroad. "So you like ponies, do you?" she asked, in a desperate attempt to change the subject.

"Of course I like ponies! We've got several at home, but my favourite is Dinglefoot Creation. Her stable name is Creo. Daddy bought her for me last year, for an awful lot of money, and already I've won so many rosettes that there's no room for them all on my bedroom door. I just keep the firsts, and throw away the rest. Daddy always says that if you don't compete to win, there's no point in competing."

Jenny had home-made paper rosettes stuck onto her bedroom door, from pretend horse shows with cut-out paper Lundy ponies. A real rosette of any colour would have been a treasured possession.

"What's your pony called?" Isabella asked. It was clear that in her world everyone had a pony or two.

"Midnight," Jenny said, without a moment's hesitation. Lying was easy, and rather fun.

"Black, I bet," said Isabella.

"No. A sort of light golden colour, with a dark mane and tail, and dark blue eyes."

"That's unusual. Is Midnight a mare or a gelding?"

"Actually, he's a stallion."

"Wow! You don't ride him, do you?"

Jenny revelled in Isabella's look of admiration. "Yes," she said. *Why* had she said that? She'd given away her greatest secret to a stranger she didn't like, just to impress her. *Why? Why? Why?*

"Wow!" said Isabella. "Is he good at jumping?"

"Oh yes, excellent. He's jumped over pretty well every wall on the island, but he prefers jumping the stiles." Well, there was no harm in telling her that, was there? Everyone knew he was good at jumping.

"That's amazing!" Isabella exclaimed. "Some of those walls are well over four feet high!"

"More like five," Jenny said.

Isabella seemed totally lost for words as they climbed back up the slope to the Castle. When they reached the top she said, "Can I ride him?"

Jenny had to think fast. "I'm afraid not. He's running out with the mares at present, and the herd could be anywhere on a fine day like today," she said, trying to sound genuinely sorry. "Would you like to see some puffins, though? There's a colony at the Battery. It isn't too far away." She prayed Midnight hadn't jumped the wall into Ackland's Moor, which he sometimes did for fun.

The girls didn't have any binoculars, and most of the puffins were sheltering in their burrows, but they saw a few.

They walked back via the Old Light.

"Is there a KP in there, too?" Isabella asked.

"PK," Jenny said. "No, it was a lighthouse a long time ago, before the South and North Lights were built, but it was pretty useless because Lundy's often capped by fog. It's used by the Lundy Field Society now."

"What's the Lundy Field Society?"

"A group of people who study all sorts of things to do with Lundy: birds, plants, insects, mammals, fish, rocks, archaeology - you name it, they study it."

"Sounds like a waste of time, to me," Isabella said.

Jenny had planned to drop in on the Old Light, as she often did on her travels, but she decided to give it a miss.

By the time they got back to the village they were tired and dizzy from the strong sun. Mrs Hamilton was serving teas in the Tea Garden, so they stopped for a quick drink and some biscuits.

Mrs Hamilton's main job was managing the Manor Farm Hotel but, like all the islanders, she turned her hand to anything that needed doing. Hotel guests were sometimes amazed to see the immaculate Mrs Hamilton sorting sheep or setting seed potatoes ready for the plough to turn in.

As they walked down the Beach Road, Isabella said, "Thanks for showing me around. I'm sorry we didn't see Midnight, but I must admit I've enjoyed today more than I thought I would."

"Thanks for getting me out of working in the kitchens all day," Jenny replied. She felt absurdly pleased that Isabella now seemed to like her. All her instincts told her she really shouldn't like Isabella.

The Landing Beach was a hive of activity. A couple of boats transported small groups of visitors from a tractor-pulled landing stage to the steamer. This involved a lot of effort, and most of the islanders were helping in some way. As the girls neared the Landing Beach, Isabella scanned the crowd. "Daddy!" she shouted.

Several people turned round to look. A large, powerfully built man dressed in a suit stood a short distance from the main crowd on the beach. He ground his cigarette into the shingle, pointed to the landing stage and started walking purposefully towards it.

"Looks like I'd better go. Good luck with the jumping," said Isabella. "Perhaps I'll see you at a show sometime." Then she hurried to join her father.

Jenny watched the Wagstaffs make their way to the landing stage. The people in the queue let them go to the front, without question. Mr Wagstaff looked as if he owned the place.

The real owner, Mr Bonham, blended in with the islanders in his shorts and open-necked shirt as he helped people aboard, and wished them a safe journey.

I didn't really lie, Jenny told herself. Midnight's practically mine, anyway. I just told a few white lies which made Isabella much friendlier. Besides, we'll never see each other again, so no harm's done.

CHAPTER THREE

Jenny woke early. The rising summer sun shone like a spotlight on her bed. She lay still for a while, listening to the sound of her bedroom curtains shifting in the gentle breeze. Faraway noises wafted in – gulls, birds, farm animals – and she savoured the wonderful feeling that a perfect day lay ahead. No day-visitors and no work, just beautiful weather and the whole island to explore. What could be better? She got up, tiptoed into the kitchen, quietly gathered together some food and left a note saying she'd be back in time for supper. Then she slipped out of the house before her father woke up and found her a job.

Once outside, Jenny went over to the farmyard to feed her pet animals: six bantams, her tame goat called Ermintrude, and two orphan lambs called Dot and Dash. The lambs had been adorable when they'd been babies struggling for survival, but they weren't adorable any more. Since March they'd grown into noisy, demanding little thugs who frequently knocked her over in their rush to get at the milk bottle. Feeding them was now a chore rather than a pleasure, as her father had warned her it would be when she'd begged him to let her keep them. Her determination to prove him wrong was the main thing which kept her feeding them religiously twice a day.

As soon as she'd seen to her animals, Jenny hurried away to find the ponies. They were by the Old Hospital ruins, lazing in the morning sun. Kit still hadn't foaled. She looked as round as a barrel, standing nose-to-tail with her best friend, Dunlin. The foals lay flat-out while their mothers stood over them, heavy-eyed and droopy-lipped. A few drowsy insects buzzed between the wildflowers, waiting for the day to begin in earnest. The grass glistened with dewdrops. Seabirds called in the distance.

Rosie, who was the oldest mare and seemed to be the boss, stood next to Midnight. They were always together. Rosie was strawberry roan, with no white markings at all.

Midnight stirred as Jenny approached. He raised his head, and his nostrils flickered in recognition.

"Hello, handsome," she said, stroking his shoulder. "Guess what? I dreamed I owned you last night, and we entered a show-jumping competition and beat Isabella! We got a great big red rosette, and she chucked away her blue one."

Midnight lowered his head and relaxed while she talked to him and rubbed his sleek summer coat, working in small circles down his neck and along his back. He always went into a sleepy trance when she did that, with a blissful look on his face.

"Perhaps one day I really will own you. Would you like that?" Jenny said. "Actually, I suppose you don't realise you're owned by *anyone*. We humans are peculiar creatures, aren't we? What gives us the right to own things and decide what happens to them? Horses, dogs, farm animals, land – whole islands, even. It's so odd, when you think about it."

Midnight blew gently through his nose, and rested a hind leg.

"If horses *do* think they own things, I bet you reckon you own this place," Jenny said.

Her arm began to ache. She stopped rubbing Midnight, and walked back to the track so she could sit on a stone.

He followed, as if she were leading him.

She started running, to see what would happen, and he trotted after her. She ran in circles, trying to catch him out, but he followed like a shadow, stopping when she stopped and tagging along when she moved. Magic!

Looking up, Jenny caught sight of two people walking along the track towards them.

"Shoo! Shoo!" she hissed, waving her arms and jumping up and down. She couldn't let anyone see Midnight being so tame.

Alarmed by her sudden madness, Midnight shied away, kicking up his heels, and dashed back to the mares and foals.

The taller person ran towards her. As he came nearer, she realised it was Albert.

"Are you all right, Jenny?" he called. "You're not hurt, are you?"

For a moment she couldn't understand what he was talking about, but then she realised it must have looked as if Midnight were chasing her. "Yes, I'm fine, thanks. I think I must have got a bit close," she answered.

Albert reached her. "Thank goodness for that," he said. "You really shouldn't get too near the ponies, you know. Mares with foals can be dangerous, and that stallion's a devil." He turned to the teenage boy behind him. "Jenny, this is my son, Ben. He came over on the boat yesterday. He's working here for the summer, but Mr Hamilton's given him the day off, so he can get to know the place."

Ben had his father's bright blue eyes and friendly smile, but otherwise Jenny wouldn't have known they were related. Albert was tall and slim, with a full head of well-cut silvery hair. Ben had floppy fair hair and a stocky, solid body. Like a well-built pony, Jenny thought approvingly. She guessed he was about sixteen years old.

"Do you always get up this early?" Ben asked.

"Sometimes. I wanted to see if Kit had foaled, but she hasn't," Jenny replied. "What about you?"

"Father's on watch after dinner, so I had to get up early for a grand tour of the island."

"We're heading to the North Light for some breakfast," said Albert. "Do you want to come?"

"Yes, please!" Jenny said. The day was turning out even better than expected.

Granite grit crunched beneath their feet as they walked along the track to the North Light. Albert strode on ahead, occasionally stopping to watch birds through his binoculars, leaving Jenny and Ben to talk.

"Shouldn't you be at school?" Jenny asked, and instantly regretted sounding so bossy.

Ben laughed. "Not any more. I left as soon as I could. I wouldn't have got any O Levels, anyway."

Having been brought up to believe that a good education was essential, Jenny was shocked and rather impressed. She hadn't realised it was possible to leave school without a single qualification, and she couldn't help admiring Ben for his apparent lack of concern.

"What's your excuse?" Ben asked.

"My excuse for what?"

"For not being at school."

"This is my school. I'm taught by Mrs Hamilton. She runs the Hotel."

"I think I've met her. Large, efficient and scary?"

"That's the one," Jenny giggled. "Once she made me rinse my mouth out with soap and water, for swearing."

"You're joking!" exclaimed Ben.

"She's not that bad, really. She's very strict, but pretty fair, and she works awfully hard. Dad says the island would grind to a halt without her. She's a good teacher, too. I got a scholarship to St Anne's because of her, worst luck."

"What? St Anne's, Bideford?"

"Yes, why?"

"Crikey! The poshest school in North Devon! What are you hoping to be? A brain surgeon?"

It had never occurred to Jenny that she would have to *be* anything. As far as she was concerned, she'd go to St Anne's, learn how to ride and then live on Lundy forever. She'd probably run the Stores or something. "I haven't really given it much thought," she said. "Definitely not a brain surgeon, though. Ugh! What about you? What are you going to be?"

"A farmer. A farmer with a boat, though. I could never be far from the sea."

"Just like Dad! Perhaps you'll have to take over his job here when he retires, although that won't be for ages. He says he could never live anywhere else. I suppose everyone who lives here feels like that."

"How many people live here, then, apart from the lighthouse-keepers?"

Jenny counted on her fingers. "There's me, Dad, Mr and Mrs Hamilton, Mark (in the Tavern) and Mary (in the Stores), Duncan (who's a builder, amongst other things), Sheila (the cook), Sue (who does cleaning, mostly), Daisy (that's just his nickname – his real name is Dave, and he does lots of different jobs), James (the Field Society warden) and old Batty (Major Bathurst) at Tibbett's. Twelve all year-round, I think, or seventeen if you count the Bonhams. Then from Easter onwards, lots more people come and go: Mr Bonham's brother and his family, other guests at Millcombe, Field Society members, visitors in the

Hotel and the cottages, fishermen and sailors, seasonal workers – all sorts."

"Nice to know I'm an *all sorts*."

"Well, it's better than being a bluebottle."

"What's a bluebottle?"

"A day-tripper. They come in like a swarm of flies, buzz around for a bit and then buzz off." Jenny gave a demonstration, buzzing up the track.

Ben followed, laughing.

They soon caught up with Albert.

"The wildlife's up early this morning!" he said in a low voice, pointing up the track.

Jenny immediately saw what he meant, and giggled. "Here comes Batty," she whispered to Ben.

A large, grey-haired gentleman with a bushy white beard marched along the track towards them. Despite the promise of a hot day, he wore a thick tweed jacket, a shirt and tie, plus-fours, long green socks and walking boots. A huge pair of binoculars hung around his neck.

"What-ho, Jenny! Morning, Albert! We're all up at sparrow's fart this morning, by the looks of it!"

Jenny caught Ben's eye, and they both snorted with suppressed laughter.

"Good morning, Major Bathurst. May I introduce my son, Ben? He's working here for a few weeks. Ben, this is Major Bathurst, who lives at Tibbett's – the old Admiralty lookout over there."

"What-ho, Ben! Welcome to the madhouse!" Batty roared, and he carried on towards the village.

On Tibbett's Hill, the whole of the north end of Lundy opened up before them, like the deck of a vast ship.

As they carried on northwards, the tussocky grass gradually gave way to granite outcrops encrusted with dry heather and lichens. A fire in the 1930s had destroyed most of the peaty soil, and the land was taking a long time to recover. It was bleak and wild, and Jenny loved it.

They were talking so much that it seemed no time at all before they were through the North Light's narrow entrance between the rocks, and descending the long cascade of steps down to the lighthouse.

The keepers must be pretty desperate for a drink and some company when they walk from here to the Tavern at night, Jenny thought.

Albert knocked on the pristine door of the North Light, and then walked in before it was answered.

"Come in! No need to knock!" a voice shouted from a room at the end of the white corridor.

The lighthouses were another world; a ship-shape, impersonal world of paint, shiny brass and squeaky-clean glass.

"You couldn't have come at a better moment, the kettle's just boiled," Gareth said, as he took a blue enamel kettle off the cooker.

Its ear-splitting whistle subsided to a soft whine.

Gareth handed round heavy mugs of tea, and put a bowl of sugar lumps and a jug of condensed milk on the table. Then he went along to the foot of the stone stairs. "Cup of tea, John?" he shouted. "John's on duty at the moment, and Neil's having a kip," he explained on his return.

"No I'm not. I heard the kettle. Got visitors? Wow, a party!" Neil said, yawning and rubbing his eyes.

John followed him into the kitchen.

"Good to see you, Neil. How's life, John?" Albert asked.

"Boring. Weather's too good."

Albert laughed. "Make the most of it," he said. "It looks as if we're going to get the tail end of that storm from America in the next day or so."

Tea made with condensed milk will always remind me of lighthouses, Jenny thought, savouring every mouthful. A deep happiness settled inside her as they sat round the table, talking about the weather, boats, fishing, gardening, which birds were nesting where, news from the village – all sorts of things. Gareth raided the Trinity House supplies and treated his visitors to exotic food, like tinned pineapple. They even tried a packet of something called Vesta Curry, which Gareth said was the latest thing in quick meals. Jenny didn't like it much, but Ben thought it was delicious, even at breakfast time.

Before they left, John took Jenny and Ben up the tower to the lantern room.

"As you can see, I've put the safety blinds down," he said. "When the sun's shining on the lenses, the rays are so powerful they can set your clothes on fire."

Even with the blinds down, the air was stifling.

Ben walked round the massive boat-shaped lantern, fascinated by every detail. "This must weigh a ton!" he said.

"Over three-and-a-half tons, if you count the framework. Although it's heavy, the lantern moves ever-so easily because it's in that trough of mercury. It makes one complete revolution every sixteen minutes."

"What's this big handle for?" Ben asked.

"That's for winding up the mechanism," John replied. "It works a bit like a grandfather clock, see? The weights hang in a cast iron tube which runs down the centre of the tower. Unfortunately this tower's a bit short, so we have to rewind the whole thing every few hours. It's hard work, I can tell you."

"And where does the light come from?"

"A PVB – a paraffin vaporiser burner. It sits in the centre, see? The compressed paraffin...."

Jenny left them talking, and wandered round the

lantern, marvelling at the sheer scale of it all. She was afraid to touch anything in case she left untidy fingerprints. It seemed everything in a lighthouse had a hard surface, polished to perfection.

She joined them again. "Even on a calm day like today the wind makes a noise up here, doesn't it?" she said. "It must be scary in a storm."

"It certainly tests your nerve on occasion," John replied. "After a while you can tell the force of the wind just by the noise it makes against the glass. If it's humming, it's force five, and then the pitch increases at six, seven and eight." He gave convincing impressions of the noise at those wind speeds and, mercifully, stopped at gale force eight. Then he showed them how to enter a weather observation in the log book, which the keeper on watch had to do every three hours.

Perhaps I'll be a lighthouse-keeper, Jenny thought. I'll be at the South Light, though, because it's closer to the village.

They left just before noon. Outside it had turned into a blisteringly hot day.

"How about going to Brazen Ward for a swim?" Jenny suggested.

"I can't. It's my watch soon," said Albert. "Why don't you go along, Ben?"

It was as if Jenny had known Ben all her life. Talking was easy; silences were easy – just being with him was easy. It didn't seem to matter he was nearly four years older.

They navigated their way down the steep zigzag path to Brazen Ward. It appeared to lead nowhere but, like so many paths on Lundy, promised by its existence to lead somewhere.

A mournful, watery sing-song floated up from the cove, rising and then falling away again. Looking down, they saw dark torpedo-shaped animals on the rocks below, which occasionally splashed into the water and transformed into graceful, grey fish-like creatures.

"I hope you don't mind seals," Jenny said.

"Of course not, but will the seals mind us?" Ben replied.

The seals didn't seem to mind them at all. Jenny and Ben swam in their T-shirts and shorts, and emerged, dripping and laughing, to sit on the smooth rocks. All around them seal heads popped out of the water, wide-eyed and curious.

Ben sat with his arms hugging his knees. "This is great. It's like the Garden of Eden."

"Without the serpent," Jenny replied.

"Eh?"

"There aren't any reptiles on Lundy, so a serpent's out of the question, I'm afraid."

"Oh, well that's even better, isn't it? The Garden of Eden, without a snake to mess things up. Perfect."

Jenny lay back on the hot rock, totally content. Waves lapped gently just below her feet, and gulls wheeled and called to each other – white silhouettes soaring against the shimmering blue sky. Perfect was the right word.

By the time they'd scrambled up to the top again the strong sun had dried their salty clothes to a crisp, and they were longing for another swim. They sat down for a rest.

"Fancy *owning* all this!" Ben said.

"I know, wouldn't it be great?" Jenny replied. "Although I think all of us islanders feel we do own it in a way – or perhaps it owns us. Either way, it sort of becomes a part of you after a while. But to *really* own it would be most peculiar, wouldn't it? I wonder if Mr Bonham wakes up every morning and says, 'I own Lundy! Yippee!' I know I would."

Ben laughed. "It must be a worry sometimes, though, running a place like this. What's he like, then, this Mr Bonham?"

"He's really nice, actually, just very normal and nice." Jenny also thought he was incredibly dashing, but she didn't say so. "He inherited Lundy when old Mr Bonham died a few years ago, so he hasn't owned it that long. He has to work in London most of the time, but he comes here as much as he can – sometimes all the way from London just for a weekend! When he's here, he joins in with whatever needs doing, like a proper islander. I'm sure he'd live here if he could, but I don't think Mrs Bonham likes it quite so much. She misses London a lot, and she has to look after the children when she's here. Their old nanny refuses to come now, ever since she had to land at Jenny's Cove in an easterly gale."

Ben smiled. "How old are the children, then?"

"William's about four. He's okay, but he asks questions the whole time. Then there's Camilla, who's six. I like Camilla, she's sweet. She dotes on Hector, and I can't think why. He's about ten, I think, and he's horrible."

"Horrible Hector!" Ben said, thoroughly amused. "Why is he so horrible?"

Jenny sighed. "Oh, lots of reasons. For instance, I caught him throwing stones at the ponies to make them run, so I threw a stone at *him* to show him what it felt like, and my aim was rather too good. Needless to say, he made out I'd been throwing stones at him for no reason, so I got into trouble."

"Serious trouble?"

"Not really. I think his parents knew he hadn't told the full story, so I got off with a lecture from Mrs Hamilton."

"That, to me, would be serious trouble!" Ben said.

On their way home they took a detour to find the ponies, which were grazing to the south-west of Pondsbury. Kit still hadn't foaled.

Jenny tried to hide her disappointment. The arrival of Kit's foal would have rounded off a perfect day. "Come on, I'll show you Jenny's Cove and the earthquakes," she said.

They picked their way through the jagged crevasses of the earthquake zone, and sat on a grassy ledge overlooking Jenny's Cove.

"Is Jenny's Cove named after you?" Ben asked.

Jenny laughed. "No, of course not! It was named after a ship which sank here in the eighteenth century, full of treasure," she said. "Actually, it's the other way round – I was named after this cove. This used to be Mum and Dad's favourite place."

"How come it isn't any more?"

Jenny didn't even hesitate. "Mum died. She slipped and fell off a cliff when she was helping with a bird survey."

Ben looked her in the eye, direct and sincere. "How awful! How old were you?"

"I was five-and-a-half."

"Do you remember her?"

"Oh yes, especially in my dreams. Sometimes they're so real that I wake up thinking she's still alive. I hate it when that happens. It's awful for Dad, too. I think he works all the time to block out the memories. He even sold Mum's pony, a beautiful Lundy mare called Puffin, to someone on the mainland because he couldn't bear to see her every day. Poor Puffin! It wasn't her fault."

Jenny thought fleetingly about Isabella. How different Ben was! He allowed her to be herself. Talking about anything was easy with Ben, even talking about Mum.

They sat, looking out over Jenny's Cove, and talked.

CHAPTER FOUR

Ben didn't start work the following day, and the steamer from Ilfracombe was cancelled. As Albert had predicted, the storm from America arrived as a south-westerly gale.

People who ventured out were sent scudding up the High Street, and had to fight their way down again, inch by inch. By lunchtime, most had managed to tack their way to the Tavern, where they stayed for most of the afternoon.

The wind howled round Jenny's cottage, lifting the curtains even though the windows were fastened. The glass panes creaked and rattled.

She spent the morning reading. When she was in the middle of a good story she couldn't bear to put it down. Her current book was a particularly exciting adventure story for boys, which Albert had lent her.

"Are you coming to the Tavern, Jenny?" her father called from the kitchen. "I've finished up outside, so I thought I might pop in for a while."

The Tavern was great fun sometimes, but Jenny knew it would be packed. Being the summer, a lot of extra people were on the island. She had visions of being squashed in a crowd of adults she didn't know very well. They'd all be talking, smoking and drinking above her.

"No thanks, Dad," she replied. She wanted to finish the

story. Then she'd try to sort out her stamps.

Jenny had started her collection with Lundy stamps, but recently she'd branched out into foreign ones. Mr Hamilton received letters from all over the world, usually enquiring about Lundy and its famous stamps, and he'd started giving the envelopes to her. She loved having them, but it was difficult to keep such a wide variety of stamps in order.

"Will you be all right by yourself?" her father asked, looking round the door. "Whatever you do, don't go outside while I'm gone. I'll leave Meg in the kitchen, for company."

Jenny didn't even look up. She didn't want to lose her place on the page. "I'll be fine. Have a good time," she said.

"Bye, then. I won't be long. Be good."

The front door closed with a bang.

The wind increased from a howl to a scream. It hammered against the windows, like an outraged giant trying to get in. Jenny feared the glass would break. She wondered what sort of noise the wind was making against the glass in the lighthouses. It didn't seem possible that only yesterday she'd been in the North Light tower, and it had been lovely weather. She felt very alone all of a sudden, and longed for the companionship of the overcrowded Tavern.

It isn't *that* far to walk, and I'll be sheltered by walls for most of the way, Jenny thought. She went into the kitchen to find Meg, who sprang up from her bed by the cooker, wagging her tail so enthusiastically that it made her whole body squirm.

"Hello, old girl. Coming to the Tavern with me, eh?" Jenny said, putting on her coat and boots. She opened the door.

Bang! The door flew inwards and sent her flying. Her head hit the hard, cold flagstones.

Wind hurtled into the cottage, breathing life into everything. Coats leapt off their pegs, chairs jumped up and crashed down, the kitchen table turned over, bits of paper flew about like seagulls and crockery fell off the dresser and smashed onto the floor. Meg whined and tried to hide behind the upturned table.

Jenny crawled to the door, desperate to close it as soon as possible. Heave! It closed a little. Heave! A little bit more. Heave! The latch clicked into place, but the wind rattled it angrily. She pushed the large iron bolt home, to make sure. Her head hurt. She sat with her back against the door, trying to recover from the shock.

Meg navigated her way through the wreckage, wagging her tail uncertainly, and licked Jenny's face.

"Good girl, Meg. It's okay. I'm all right, really I am," Jenny said, hugging Meg's bony, hairy body. She smelt of sheep droppings.

Flash! Kerboom!

Jenny jumped with fright. Meg yelped and dived for cover again. Hailstones showered down, smashing against the cottage with such force that Jenny was sure it would disintegrate. She joined Meg, and held her tight until the thunderstorm passed and the clatter of hail on the roof gave way to the patter of raindrops.

The kitchen was never tidy at the best of times, but now it looked like a disaster zone. Jenny made a valiant attempt to clear it up.

As the wind and rain died down, a new sound drifted into the room – the penetrating, intermittent boom of the South Light foghorn. Jenny looked out of the window, and saw nothing but grey.

I hope the ponies are okay, she thought. How could any animal survive a storm like that? Especially those poor little foals – the wind was strong enough to blow them straight over the cliffs. Oh, I do hope Kit hasn't had her foal!

"Come on, Meg. Time to find Dad," she said, pulling on her boots again. She opened the door cautiously, and they stepped out into the gloom.

On impulse Jenny turned right, away from the village and the safety of the Tavern. She had to check the ponies. They were bound to be in the quarries, so it wouldn't take long.

The air was thick with moisture. A warm breeze swirled the mist around, giving crazy impressions of movement and direction. Her bruised head throbbed painfully, and she felt rather sick. She trudged on, guided by some sort of inner auto-pilot.

The ponies weren't near the Quarter Wall gate.

They weren't in any of the quarries.

Jenny searched the east side of the island between the Quarter and Halfway walls, but found only cattle.

Perhaps they'd pushed a gate open, or jumped out. Perhaps they'd been moved. The sensible thing would be to go back and ask Dad.

Jenny didn't feel sensible. She felt panicky. Something was wrong. Maybe her worst fears had been realised, and they'd all been blown over the cliffs into the sea. Surely the ponies wouldn't have stayed on the west side in a south-westerly storm? She'd have to look.

Keeping the Quarter Wall on her left, she walked over the tussocky grass and bracken to the west side of the island. It was heavy going.

Meg padded along beside her, giving her the courage to carry on.

Joining the path which ran along the west side, she headed north, still peering intently into the curtains of mist for the outline of a pony.

Nothing. Absolutely nothing.

The ground dipped round some rocks and became lumpy. Jenny knew they'd reached the earthquake zone. Meg crouched down, body quivering.

"What is it, Meg?"

Meg growled, and kept staring straight ahead. Her hackles rose. She growled again, low and menacing.

A shiver ran through Jenny, and she felt goose pimples rising over her body.

The earth shook.

"Oh no!" she thought. "*An earthquake!*"

Midnight galloped out of the mist. He galloped straight at Meg, head down and ears back.

She yelped and fled.

Nostrils flaring and head held high, Midnight returned, trotting straight at Jenny.

Her heart pounded against her ribs. Should she run or stand her ground? A sheer drop of several metres lay behind her. Falling down it would be like falling from the first floor of a house.

Jenny stood her ground. "Whoa! Steady!" she said, spreading her arms.

Midnight slid to a stop in front of her, snorting and tossing his head.

Tentatively, Jenny reached out and touched him. She knew he recognised her, but he still looked agitated.

"There's a good boy. What's the matter?"

Midnight's ears pricked, and his nostrils fluttered.

Looking up, Jenny saw the dark grey outline of a pony coming through the mist, then another and another. They looked enormous, like great ghost horses. With relief, she realised they were the mares. Mist often made things seem larger than life.

More mares appeared, shadowed by their foals. The

foals looked wet and cold, but alive.

Jenny counted them, fourteen mares and ten foals in all. She counted again, to see who was missing. Kit.

Midnight whinnied. It was powerful and heartfelt; his whole body shook with the effort.

A shrill whinny answered him. Kit was nearby, but where?

Slowly and carefully, Jenny started to navigate her way between the jumbled mass of faults and fissures which slumped towards the sea. She could hear waves pounding against the cliffs far below.

Kit stood at the edge of a steep-sided trench, pawing the ground.

Frightened of what she would see, Jenny peered into the trench. A long white object lay below on some stony turf. The object looked like a foal.

Oh no! Jenny slithered, and eventually fell, down the side of the trench, ripping her clothes and skin in the process. She ignored the stinging pain. All she could think about was reaching the foal. There was a chance, after all. The smallest, tiniest chance, wasn't there? Just a *chance* it was still alive.

As she reached the foal, it lifted its head, squealed in alarm, tried to get up, tripped over a rock and fell back awkwardly.

It's alive! Jenny thought. It's impossible to imagine something so frail could have survived such a fall. "It's okay, I won't hurt you. I'm your friend," she whispered. Gently, she stroked the wet skin on its bony little body. The foal tried to stand up again.

She held it steady while it balanced precariously on spindly legs, twitching and shivering with the effort.

At least there don't seem to be any broken bones. Not even a cut, Jenny thought. Oh, and you've got blue eyes, like Midnight!

The foal's legs crumpled, and it sank to the ground again.

I'll have to go and get Dad, Jenny thought. He'll know what to do.

The sides of the trench were steep and crumbly, and it was blocked at each end by vertical walls of rock. Jenny walked up and down, looking for the best way out. Slowly, the awful truth dawned on her; there was no way out! She tried several places, but it was no good. She was well-and-truly stuck.

Jenny said a lot of words which Mrs Hamilton wouldn't have approved of, and went back to the foal. "We'll just have to wait for a search party, little one. I'm sure it won't be long." She wished she believed her own words. Dad was always scolding her for going out exploring without telling anyone. If he came home and found her gone, he'd just think she'd gone out for a walk.

The foal lay on its side, exhausted, eyes half-closed. Jenny noticed it was a girl. By the look of her navel, she was only a few hours old.

"Gale," she said. "I'll call you Gale, because you were born in one."

Jenny took off her coat and put it over Gale. Then she sat on a slab of rock by the foal's head, and stroked her neck and her wispy mane.

The mist cleared, and small patches of blue appeared between the clouds. Midnight and Kit paced the treacherous ground above, occasionally looking over the side and snorting or whinnying. Although they were no help, Jenny felt comforted by their presence. She talked and sang to the ponies, and tried not to worry about being stuck. She tried not to worry that the foal needed milk urgently. It seemed to be getting weaker. She tried not to worry, but she couldn't help it.

The clouds above became puffy and edged with orange. Sunset wasn't far off.

"Jenny! Jenny!" Dad's voice!

"Look! There's some ponies." Ben's voice.

"Help! I'm here!" Jenny shouted.

Gale twitched with fright at the sudden noise.

"Jenny? Are you there?" Mr Hamilton's voice this time.

The shock waves from thundering hooves juddered through the rocks.

"Watch out, Ben! Here comes that stallion! Oh, no! He's going to attack Meg! Quick!"

Bang! Bang!

"Midnight! Dad! Midnight!" Jenny screamed.

"Jenny! Where are you?"

"Here! What have you done to Midnight? Is he OK?"

"He's fine. We scared him off, that's all. Thank goodness

we've found you! Are you okay?" Her father's head appeared over the edge, silhouetted against the sky. He caught sight of Jenny, and swore loudly.

Jenny smiled as best she could. "Mrs Hamilton really wouldn't approve of your language!" she said.

Soon the other islanders arrived, summoned by the sound of Mr Hamilton's shotgun. There were lots of voices, strong arms lifting, loud noises and shouting. Then a bumpy ride on the trailer followed by hot chocolate, biscuits and bed with hot water bottles.

Jenny asked about Gale constantly.

"It's OK, Jenny. We'll look after her," her father kept saying.

"She needs Kit's milk."

"I know. Don't you worry."

Finally, exhausted, Jenny drifted off to sleep.

CHAPTER FIVE

When Jenny woke up it was pitch-black and completely quiet. Shouldn't she be worried about something? She rolled over. Ouch! Why did she ache all over?

"Gale!" she said out loud.

She stretched out her arm - ouch, again - and felt for the torch on the floor beside her bed. She turned it on and squinted at her watch. Half-past-three in the morning.

Trying to ignore her protesting muscles, she carefully got out of bed and hobbled around, collecting and putting on clothes as quickly as possible.

This must be what it's like to be old, she thought. Suddenly everything's difficult - even simple things, like putting on socks.

By fading torchlight, Jenny crept through the kitchen, out of the cottage and over to the farmyard. The air felt cool and crisp. Stars peppered the sky.

Thin slivers of light shone from around the shippen door, leading to the old cattle stalls. She walked over and peered through the crack between door and doorframe. It was hard to see in the semi-darkness, but what she saw didn't look like a foal at all. It looked like a goat.

"Maah!" it went.

"Be quiet, Ermintrude. I'm trying to sleep," said a voice.

"Ben? Is that you?"

"Jenny? What are you doing? You're supposed to be asleep!"

"I know, but I woke up again. How's the foal?" She could hardly bear to ask.

"Hang on," Ben said.

Jenny heard rustling as he got up and walked over, then clunks as he pushed back the double bolts on the door.

"You can come in and see for yourself. She's had plenty of milk, and now she's fast asleep, like you should be."

Gale lay on a thick bed of straw in the corner of the shed. Her body was covered with blankets, leaving only her head visible.

Jenny knelt beside the foal and stroked her neck. It felt warm and silky.

She felt quite faint with relief.

Ben knelt beside her. "See? She's fine. There was no need to worry."

"Maah!" Ermintrude called to her fawn-coloured kid, which was playing about in the straw.

Jenny looked at her goat. "Why's Ermintrude here? Where's Kit?"

"Well, to cut a long story short, the foal was far too weak to get up and suck, and we thought it would be killed if we'd left it with its mother because she wouldn't calm down. So we brought it in here and fed it with Ermintrude's milk. Mrs Hamilton helped me. She said she'd read somewhere that goat's milk is the best substitute for mare's milk - much better than milk from a cow - so she got Ermintrude and we milked her into this rubber cleaning glove. We made a hole, with a hat pin, at the end of this finger. Look, doesn't that make a brilliant teat? Hands-up!" Ben squirted milk from the glove at Jenny.

"Eek!" Jenny grabbed at the glove, and milk spilled out over the straw. "Oops! Sorry!"

There was a shrill whinny from the shed next door.

"Now look what you've done!" Ben teased. "You've spilt the milk *and* upset Kit again!"

Jenny remembered one of the things she'd been worrying about; she wasn't sure if Gale had drunk any milk from Kit before she'd fallen into the trench. As a farmer's daughter, Jenny knew it was vital for newborn mammals to drink the first milk, or colostrum, from their mothers as soon as possible, because it protected them against disease.

"I'd better go and see if I can get some milk from Kit," Jenny said.

"*What?* You're mad!" Ben replied. "You'll get yourself killed. It's not worth it."

"But I must! Don't you see? Gale's got to have her colostrum, before it's too late."

"Gale? Don't you mean Snowy? That's what I've called her."

"Snowy! That's a silly name! She's bound to get darker in time. You can't have a golden dun pony called Snowy!"

"Almost as silly as a golden dun pony called Midnight."

Ben's teasing smile infuriated Jenny. "I called her Gale first!" she shouted in desperation, and stormed out, leaving Ben staring after her with his mouth open in disbelief.

Outside, Jenny took great gulps of air and tried to calm down. She'd liked Ben so much the first day she'd met him. In fact, she'd dreamed of having a brother like him. But now she felt so *annoyed* with him. He'd taken over all the things she should be doing. She wished she'd made the glove teat with Mrs Hamilton and given Gale her life-saving drink of Ermintrude's milk. It should have been her! *She* was the one who had waited expectantly for Gale's birth, found her - even risked her life for her. *Snowy*, indeed!

What she felt at that moment was more complicated than just being annoyed. Perhaps it was jealousy. She'd never had cause to be jealous before. Maybe if she had a brother or sister she'd feel like this a lot. Being an only child definitely had its advantages.

Kit paced around her makeshift stable, occasionally slipping at the corners where she'd scuffed the dirty straw away to expose bare stone. Her body was feathered with sweat. As Jenny watched, she raised her head and let out a shrill whinny.

An answer came immediately, like a low echo. By the sound of it, Midnight had jumped the Quarter Wall, and was trying to find her.

Jenny squeezed through the door into the stable, and shut it quickly.

The mare came to an abrupt halt.

"Hello, Kit. You are in a state, aren't you? There's a good girl. Your baby's fine, you know," Jenny said. She approached the frightened mare in the way she'd learnt with Midnight.

Before long, Kit relaxed and allowed Jenny to rub her tired, itchy body. Milk dripped down her hind legs, making little creamy puddles in the dirt – precious colostrum going to waste.

Perhaps I can milk her by hand, like Ermintrude, Jenny thought. She reached out to touch Kit's udder.

She squealed, and kicked forwards and upwards, sending Jenny reeling.

It hurt. Jenny swore as she sat on the smelly, mucky floor.

Ben had been watching over the stable door. "It looks as if your mouth isn't the only thing you'll be washing out with soap and water!" he said, and burst out laughing.

How dare he! For a moment indignation welled up inside Jenny. Then she looked down at herself and up at Ben, and laughter bubbled up instead.

He helped her out of the stable and they staggered together, laughing helplessly, back to the shippen.

"Here, I've got a surprise for you," Ben said as he opened the door.

With tentative, dainty steps Gale tottered up to Jenny, and nuzzled her hopefully.

Jenny didn't think she'd ever felt such love for anything. "She's looking for some milk," she whispered. "Do you think we dare try her with Kit?"

"Well, we'll have to sooner or later," said Ben.

They decided that Kit's stable would be too dirty for a foal, so they put Ermintrude in a different shed, closed the yard gate, opened Gale's door and Kit's door, stood back and prayed hard.

Kit rushed out madly, skidding round the yard in the cold half-light, whinnying frantically. Midnight's ardent, ever-closer replies didn't calm the situation at all.

We shouldn't have done this. Kit won't recognise Gale. She'll reject her, thought Jenny miserably. They've been parted too long.

A tiny, shrill whinny came from the shippen.

Kit slithered to a halt. She stared intently at the open double door, and her nostrils flickered. Then she walked forwards hesitantly, drawn by the possibility that the thing she wanted most in the world was inside, but fearful of the unknown.

The foal whinnied again.

Kit's answer was rumbling and tender as she went into the shed.

It was too late to do anything now, except hope for the best.

Jenny and Ben listened anxiously for squeals and bangs, but only gentle rustles and horsey murmurings came out of the shed, so they tiptoed closer to have a look.

Gale was nursing with eager sucking noises, her fluffy silver tail swishing enthusiastically. Kit nuzzled the foal's bottom as it drank, whickering affectionately.

A big tear rolled down Jenny's face.

The peace was shattered by the arrival of Midnight, hell-bent on rescuing his mare and foal. He stood at the gate into the yard, in a frenzy of excited frustration, pawing at the bars and whinnying.

Kit spun round, knocking Gale off her feet, and whinnied eagerly in reply.

Before Ben and Jenny could decide what to do, Midnight jumped the gate from a standstill.

"Hell's bells!" Ben exclaimed. "I'm getting out of here!" He dived round to Kit's old stable. "Come on, Jenny! Hurry!"

"Did you see that? He's amazing!" Jenny said.

Midnight clattered towards the stable door where she stood.

"Come *on!*" Ben urged. "He's a killer, that horse! Everyone says so."

Jenny stood still and held out her hand. "Well, I certainly don't. He's lovely. Aren't you, boy?"

Midnight arched his neck and snorted at her, eyes blazing in the pink light of dawn. Then he walked towards her, and brushed her hand with his muzzle before greeting Kit over the stable door with happy little grunts and squeals.

Jenny started to rub his neck. He quivered, relaxing at her touch.

"Blimey!" said Ben, venturing out of his hiding place.

"I'd never have believed it!"

Midnight barged against Jenny as he shied away from Ben.

"I shouldn't come too close. He's not used to strangers."

"I can see that."

"Who says he's a killer, then?" Jenny asked.

Ben looked embarrassed. "Well, quite a few people, really. They were all talking last night, after they'd rescued you. He tried attacking us when we were getting you and Snow-I-mean-Gale out of that trench. I've never seen a horse look so evil: head down, neck snaking, teeth bared, ears flat back. He meant business, I can tell you."

Jenny laughed. "What a brave boy! He was only trying to protect us."

"*Protect* you? He nearly knocked us all down with you!"

"Don't you see? He must have thought you were trying to harm Gale, not save her. He was protecting her from vile kidnappers."

"Okay, then, what about the first time we met?"

Jenny was puzzled.

"Midnight was chasing you, don't you remember? Dad was telling everyone about that, too."

"Oh, no! He wasn't, was he? Midnight wasn't chasing me, he was *following* me*!* You actually saw the most wonderful moment – the moment he followed me for the first time. It's taken years for him to trust me that much. I spent hours watching the herd before he came up and let me touch him, and now he even lets me – oh, it's no use, you wouldn't believe me anyway."

"Try me."

"He lets me ride him."

"What, properly? With a saddle and bridle?"

Jenny sighed wistfully. "No, I haven't even got a head-collar. I just hop on his back and ride him around when he's grazing with the herd sometimes. I can't steer him or anything."

"Cripes! That sounds horribly dangerous. Does your Dad know?"

"No, of course not. Nobody knows – except you. You won't tell anyone, will you? I'm afraid they'll stop me."

"From the way they were talking last night, that'll be the least of your worries. If they can catch him, they're planning on shipping him to the mainland. They've been trying to for some time, apparently, because all the ponies are becoming too closely related. They want to get a new stallion in."

Jenny was horrified. "We'd better get him out of here fast, then, before anyone wakes up! If you open the gate, I'll drive him out."

Ben got to the gate, turned back and hissed frantically, "Your Dad's coming! I'll try to stall him while you hide Midnight!"

Easier said than done! Jenny looked around the yard in a panic, but saw no easy hiding place for a wild stallion she couldn't lead. Her only hope was the shippen, with Kit and Gale. It was a risk, but there was no option. She opened the door.

Kit made to rush out, but then remembered her foal was inside, so rushed back in, hotly followed by Midnight.

Jenny slammed the doors shut behind the ponies, and forced the rusty bolts home just as Robert Medway walked in through the gate, followed by Ben making 'I'm sorry' signs.

There was a terrible commotion inside the shed: banging, sliding, squealing scraping and a thudding noise, like falling rocks. Then a few scuffles, a whinny, and silence.

"Good God! Is everything all right in there?" Robert

asked, rushing over. "Open the door, Jenny! Quickly!"

Jenny fumbled with the stubborn bolts. She was pretty certain everything wasn't all right. Gale had probably been trampled to death, apart from anything else. She flung the top door open and said, "You look, Dad. I can't bear to. I'm sorry, it was a stupid idea."

Robert peered into the dusty shed. "All well, as far as I can see. She's a bonny little thing, isn't she?"

"What? But..."

"Are you okay, Jenny? You seem a bit delirious. Perhaps you should go back to bed."

Perhaps I *have* gone potty, Jenny thought as she, too, looked into the shippen. She could see Kit and Gale standing at the far end, apparently unharmed. Midnight had vanished. At the back there was a wall which had fallen down in a storm, and had been repaired to a height of about seven feet. Beyond, there was a field called Pig's Paradise. Kit looked towards Pig's Paradise, and whinnied.

He can't have - he must have! Midnight had jumped the wall.

CHAPTER SIX

Mrs Hamilton liked nothing better than a party; birthday parties were her speciality, and her cakes, legendary.

Jenny's thirteenth birthday party was a Friday lunchtime barbecue on the Landing Beach. Everyone on the island was invited, residents and visitors alike. Fortunately it wasn't a boat day.

By midday it seemed as if the entire population of the island was on the beach, drinking, talking, swimming and cooking sausages over a driftwood fire. The sun shone down on them from a cloudless sky.

This is the best birthday ever, Jenny thought as she joined the party. It's such a pity Dad can't come because he's too busy turning the hay.

He'd given her a riding hat, a yellow polo neck, some creamy-coloured jodhpurs and a big birthday hug at breakfast time, and had then rushed off to the hay field, apologising over and over again for abandoning her on her birthday. Jenny knew he'd had no option; every hour counted when making hay.

Anyway, she'd still had a lovely morning. Mr and Mrs Hamilton had completed the riding outfit with smart brown leather riding boots, and Albert had invited her to morning tea at the South Light, where he'd given her a book. Then, on her way down to the beach, Mr Bonham had invited her into Millcombe to present her with a whole sheet of Lundy stamps.

"I found these in a drawer in my late father's desk when I was having a bit of a clear-out," he'd said. "I know you collect Lundy stamps, so I thought you might like them. They could be quite valuable, I suppose. I'm afraid I've never been terribly interested in the philatelic side of things – Mr Hamilton's the man to ask. If you'd like them, I'll keep them safe here, and you can collect them after your party."

Of course, Jenny said she would like them, and had thanked Mr Bonham very much.

As she arrived at the beach, other presents were given to her: a drawing, sweets, an interesting shell, a beautifully carved piece of driftwood.... Everyone gave her some sort of gift, except Ben.

Jenny told herself she shouldn't mind. Presents weren't important. The fact that Ben was there should be enough. It was wrong of her to expect anything, and she felt ashamed for being disappointed.

After lunch, most of the men – including Ben – left to help carry the hay, and Jenny helped Mr and Mrs Hamilton clear up the party debris. The tractor and trailer were being used for haymaking, so everything had to be carried up the Beach Road by hand.

Jenny walked with Mr Hamilton. He obviously wanted to concentrate on breathing rather than talking, which suited Jenny fine; she always felt shy in his company. All the islanders liked and respected Mr Hamilton, but they were careful not to cross him. He didn't suffer fools gladly, and had a reputation for speaking his mind.

At Millcombe Jenny suddenly remembered her stamps, and went into the house to get them.

Mr Hamilton seemed only too glad to stop for a breather.

Jenny ran back down the drive, anxious not to keep him waiting. “Here they are! Mr Bonham said they could be quite valuable, and that you’d know.” She handed him the large white envelope Mr Bonham had given her to protect the stamps. It had the Bonham family crest embossed on the back.

“My dear girl!” Mr Hamilton said slowly as he looked inside. “Where on earth did he find these?”

“In the bottom of an old desk, I think. Why?”

Mr Hamilton carefully eased the stamps out of the envelope. “Well, you can replace ‘quite’ with ‘very’, for a start. *Very* valuable. I dread to think what they’d make if they were put up for auction. They’re unique, you see. This is the only sheet of these particular stamps ever printed, because they suddenly realised they’d designed the whole thing without including the name Lundy. Look.”

“Oh, yes.”

Mr Hamilton continued, “Young Jeremy is a fool! All he had to do was ask me, after all. No wonder he’s got money troubles, if he gives away valuable possessions like this! Dear me, forget I said that - heat of the moment.”

Jenny felt like a thief. “I’m so sorry! I had no idea! I’ll go and return them at once!”

She ran back up the drive. What’s worse, she thought, to return a very generous present, or to accept it knowing it’s much more valuable than was intended? The imposing front door opened before she had a chance to knock, and she nearly fell into Mr Bonham’s arms as he came out.

“Ah, Jenny! Back so soon? I was just going up to help with the haymaking. Are you going that way, too?”

“Not *quite, very!*” Jenny blurted out.

“Come again?”

"The stamps aren't 'quite' valuable. They're 'very' valuable! Mr Hamilton says so. They're 'unique'. Thank you very much, but I really can't take them. They're worth too much money."

Tall, handsome, self-assured Mr Bonham looked nearly as embarrassed as Jenny felt. He hesitated, and then said decisively, "No. It's very good of you to tell me, Jenny, and to offer to give them back, but I won't hear of it. The stamps are yours. I hope you enjoy them. And if you do ever sell them, use the money wisely for something you really want. Now, Mr Hamilton's waiting for you, and I've got some hay to carry. Maybe we'll see you later in the Tavern, eh?" He patted her kindly on the shoulder, and then turned left to go through the side entrance to Millcombe.

"T-thank you! Thank you very much indeed!" Jenny called after him, and she sprinted back to Mr Hamilton.

"Well?"

"Mr Bonham wouldn't take them back. He said they're mine to keep, or sell if I want to, which I don't, of course."

"I expected nothing less of him, but you were right to try. The trouble is, he's a true gentleman. A rare thing these days, I can tell you. He'd never go back on his word, or his gifts. His father was just the same. Well, I hope you keep them safe, my girl. And if you do ever sell them, for goodness sake consult me first."

To her great relief, when Jenny reached the Hotel, Mrs Hamilton excused her from any further work because it was her birthday. I wish every day could be my birthday, Jenny thought as she carried her presents back to the cottage in a cardboard box. She left most of them in the box, but took care to place the precious stamps in her bedside drawer. Then she dashed out again to find the ponies. Her birthday wouldn't be complete without seeing Midnight and Gale.

On the way she met the tractor with a load of hay destined for the barn.

Ben was perched on top of the load, grinning broadly and obviously loving every minute of the hot, dusty, exhausting work. Mr Bonham was up there with him, looking equally happy and very dashing in some old-fashioned tennis whites which had been demoted to farm work.

"Hello, birthday girl!" Ben called down to her. "Want a ride?"

Jenny longed to say yes, but she knew she'd be useless at hay-carting. It was all she could do to lift a bale, let alone throw it or toss it over her head with a fork. "No thanks. I'm off to see the ponies," she replied.

"Send my love to Snow-I-mean-Gale!" Ben called back.

"Okay!" Jenny didn't mind him teasing her about Gale's name any more. It had become a secret joke between them, and she rather liked it. She wished Ben would jump down from the trailer and join her. It appeared she was the only person on the whole island who wasn't working that afternoon. Usually she relished a few hours of freedom, but that afternoon she felt guilty about it – and unusually lonely.

As soon as Jenny saw the ponies, her heart lurched with fright. They were laid flat out on a patch of close-cropped grass. Even Midnight looked completely lifeless. It appeared the whole herd had been struck down by some terrible disease.

"No!" she screamed. "No! Oh, please, no!"

She ran towards them, desperately fearful, drawn like a magnet to the terrible disaster before her.

Midnight raised his head, and looked at the screaming girl running towards him. Reluctantly, he scrambled to his feet. Several other mares followed suit, rousing their foals. Jenny stood still, feeling like a fool. The herd seemed to come to life before her eyes, as if woken from a magic spell in a fairy tale. They'd only been sunbathing!

As Jenny went up to him, Midnight swished his tail and walked away with his ears back, like a grumpy old man woken from his siesta.

Gale was more forgiving. She trotted up for a cuddle, uttering short high-pitched whinnies. She was now a spirited, inquisitive foal, with a solid little body, velvet skin and shining blue eyes. Jenny adored her.

After a while Midnight wandered up. He nudged Jenny, begging for attention.

"Why, I do believe you're jealous!" she said, stroking him lovingly.

By the time Jenny left the ponies, she could no longer hear the distant drone of the tractor, and the hay field was empty – stripped bare, like a shorn sheep. The sweet smell of fresh hay hung in the air as she made her way home.

In the kitchen there was a note from her father, saying he'd gone to the Tavern. After washing quickly, and putting on her best jeans and shirt, she went to join him.

A party was already in full swing. To Jenny's slight embarrassment, she was immediately the centre of attention. Mrs Hamilton played *Happy Birthday* on the piano, and everyone sang along, followed by three cheers led by Mr Hamilton. Then Mr Hamilton sang his party piece, which the islanders called *The Hartland Song*, and they joined in the chorus with great gusto: "*And the larks they sang melodious! And the larks they sang melodious! And the larks they sang melodious at the break of the day.*"

Several others took a turn with songs, stories or poems. James, the Field Society warden, got out his guitar and played some Lonnie Donegan songs, and Albert gave a hilarious recital of *The Lion and Albert* and *The Return of Albert.*

Then Daisy got up and sang *Daisy Bell*, which had become his signature tune over the years and had resulted in his nickname. Anyone less like a girl was hard to imagine. Daisy had tattoos up his arms, a shaved head, broken teeth and a neck like a bull. He'd turn his hand to anything, and was, as Mr Hamilton put it, 'the salt of the earth'.

What Daisy lacked in musical ability he made up for with enthusiasm, and they all linked arms and sang the chorus: "*Daisy, Daisy give me your answer do! I'm half crazy, all for the love of you....*"

By this time Ben was standing next to Jenny, his arm linked with hers. She felt light-headed and happy, although she couldn't help noticing - with a twinge of disappointment - that he sang badly out of tune.

Sheila put plates of sandwiches and hot sausage rolls on the counter. Conversation subsided to a subdued murmuring as everybody began eating. Jenny and Ben found a couple of seats in the corner.

"Oh, that's better!" Ben sat down. He looked weary, and his face glowed with sunburn. There were angry red blisters on his hands.

"Still want to be a farmer?" Jenny teased.

"You bet! Today's been brilliant!"

Jenny suspected that hauling hay bales until his hands were raw had made Ben's day, not her birthday celebrations. After all, he hadn't even bothered to get her a present, had he?

Robert Medway stood up and banged on a table.

Everyone was surprised into silence; they knew he hated being the centre of attention.

"I'd like to propose a toast to my beautiful daughter, Jenny." He looked straight at her, making her blush. "You'll always be my sunshine," he said, slurring slightly, his usual reserve softened by drink. "All the very best!"

"To Jenny!" everyone chorused. "All the very best!" They drank her health enthusiastically.

"And I'd like to propose a toast to the haymakers. Thanks for all your help. It would have been a long, lonely job without you," he added.

"To the haymakers!"

Robert was enjoying himself. "And to Sheila and Mrs Hamilton for feeding us all!"

A communal cry of, "To the cooks!" nearly raised the roof.

Mrs Hamilton carried in a birthday cake with thirteen candles flickering on top. It was a work of art. She'd made it in the shape of a pony, with a golden marzipan body and chocolate mane and tail. Golden dun, like Midnight.

It was so beautiful that Jenny didn't want to cut it, but everybody was watching expectantly. She removed the candles, leaving deep, ugly craters in the marzipan. Then she closed her eyes and plunged the knife into the cake, making a fervent wish as she did so.

Happy Birthday was sung for the third time that day, louder than ever.

As Jenny opened her eyes, she realised she'd cut through the heart of her cake pony. She knew she was being silly, but it mattered terribly. Her throat went tight, and hot tears prickled her eyes. She hastily rubbed them and pulled at her eyelid, pretending an eyelash had become trapped.

"Give us a tune, Jenny!" Batty roared from the other side of the room. "How about some jolly old Scott Joplin? You're awfully good at that!"

Friendly hands pushed Jenny towards the piano, crowding in and then thinning out like a retreating wave, leaving a respectful space around the piano. Jenny sat down on the stool and spent a long time adjusting it to the right height while the nervousness she always felt before playing to an audience subsided. Without saying anything, she launched straight into her favourite ragtime tune, *The Maple Leaf Rag*, and her nerves evaporated.

The piano was so familiar that Jenny could have hit the right notes with her eyes closed. She'd been playing it since she was six, under the careful tuition of Mrs Hamilton, and she was allowed to practise whenever the Tavern was closed. When she knew Mrs Hamilton was listening, she played Mozart, Beethoven and other classical composers. When she thought she could get away with it, she switched to rag tunes, or tried to work out the tunes of pop songs she'd heard on the radio.

As she played the final chord, everybody clapped, and over the general noise Batty bellowed "Bravo! Encore!"

"This one's for Dad. It's called *You Are My Sunshine*," Jenny said.

Those who had lived on Lundy for some time could remember Jane Medway playing the same song on the same piano, with Robert singing by her side.

When the chorus came around, Robert walked over to his daughter and, to everybody's surprise, led the singing: "*You are my sunshine, my only sunshine; you make me happy when skies are grey. You'll never know, dear, how much I love you. Please don't take my sunshine away."* Robert's eyes shone with unshed tears.

The Tavern was now completely packed, so that it was difficult to move. It looked as if several people were intent on making the party last until dawn.

Jenny hugged her father and said, "Night, night. I'm off home. Thanks for a lovely birthday."

"Goodnight, love. Are you sure you'll be all right by yourself? Would you like me to come with you?"

Jenny could see he didn't want to leave. "No, I'll be fine."

"The last time you said that, we had to rescue you from the bottom of a ravine!"

Jenny laughed. "No ravines tonight, I promise."

Cool, hay-laden air greeted Jenny as she left the Tavern. The night was calm and clear, but still warm enough to feel comfortable wearing a thin shirt. She stood for a moment, looking up at the stars.

The Tavern door banged shut, making her jump. She swung round.

Ben hurried towards her. "Thank goodness you're still there! I thought you'd gone home," he said. "I've got a birthday present for you."

He'd remembered! He *did* care!

He took her hand. "Come on, it's in the Church."

Jenny waited by the heavy oak door of the Church while Ben went in to get her mysterious gift.

He returned, holding a parcel. "Let's go outside," he whispered.

"Okay," Jenny whispered back, wondering why it didn't seem right to talk normally in church.

They walked a short distance, and then Ben sat down on the grass.

Jenny sat beside him on the spongy turf.

The moon bathed everything in silvery light, washing out all the normal colours.

"Happy Birthday," Ben said, and he handed her a crinkled brown paper parcel tied up with string.

It was quite flat, but knobbly, and heavier than she'd expected. She had absolutely no idea what it could be. Trying to hide her eagerness, she eased off the string.

A tangled mass of knotted rope slid from the package and slumped onto the grass.

Jenny felt confused. Had Ben played some sort of joke on her?

"I hope you like it. I made it myself, but I think it'll work okay. I got the rope from a fisherman, in return for helping him for an afternoon. Do you like it, Jenny? Please say something!"

What on earth can I say? Jenny thought. I can't say I love it when I don't even know what it is. She lifted the rope by the largest knot, and suddenly everything fell into shape. "Oh! Thank you! It's-it's perfect!" she said. "A rope halter!"

"For Midnight," Ben added.

CHAPTER SEVEN

The sun shone from a deep blue sky, making the sea sparkle. Jenny looked longingly out of the large sash window of the Hotel bedroom she was supposed to be cleaning.

It's so unfair, she thought. I live here all year round, but just when the weather's good, the days are long and lots of people are enjoying themselves, I have to work - boring women's work, at that. Men have much more interesting jobs, with boats and tractors and animals. I wish I could work with Ben.

She couldn't stop thinking about Ben, and the halter he'd given her. It was her most prized possession - even more special than her priceless stamps or the soft yellow polo neck jumper folded carefully in her bedroom cupboard, ready and waiting for her first riding lesson. The halter was precious because Ben had made it, and had given it to her in secret. It was also precious because it held the key to Midnight's future. With it, if everything went according to plan, she would be able to tame him and show everyone what a wonderful pony he was. Then he'd be allowed to stay on Lundy forever, and she'd be able to ride him all over the island. They'd be inseparable. And if he couldn't be the herd stallion any more, perhaps he could just have Rosie and a few of the older mares for company -

the ones who weren't closely related to him. She'd keep them by the cottage, in St Helen's Field...

"Jenny! Haven't you finished that room yet? Do hurry up! Sheila needs help in the kitchen." Mrs Hamilton's head appeared round the bedroom door. "My goodness! You haven't even made the bed yet! Get a move on, child!"

Rudely awakened from her glorious daydream, Jenny leapt to the bed and hurriedly rearranged the sheets and blankets, taking care to smooth down the bits that showed. Then she rushed downstairs to the kitchen.

By evening, Jenny felt so weary her bones ached. All she really wanted to do was lie on her bed and read, but she'd promised herself she'd start training Midnight with the halter. She had no idea how long it took to break a wild pony, but she knew she should make a start as soon as possible. He had to be fully trained by the end of the summer holidays. She'd be off to school in September; her stomach cramped up every time she thought about it.

Reluctantly she got off her bed, opened the top drawer of her chest of drawers and took the halter from its hiding place under her pants, vests and socks.

The lead rope was made from the same piece of rope as the halter. Jenny wound the whole thing round her waist, and then put her anorak on, zipping it up with difficulty.

Her father was reading a *Farmer and Stockbreeder* magazine at the kitchen table, surrounded by the dirty dishes from tea. The radio crackled and whined in its efforts to pick up *The Archers* from the mainland.

Jenny edged out of her bedroom door, and crept round the side of the kitchen.

"Going out again?" Robert asked. "Don't be late. I thought you were looking rather tired at teatime." His eyes didn't leave the page he was reading.

"I'm fine. Won't be long," Jenny said quickly. Then she was out of the door, and away.

For the first time in her life, Jenny was nervous as she approached Midnight. Sensing it instantly, he snorted at the rope halter in her hand, and backed away.

Just act normally, you fool, Jenny told herself. She stood looking out to sea, ignoring Midnight and the ponies, trying to calm herself. Before long she felt warm breath on her hand. It wasn't Midnight, it was Gale.

As Jenny cuddled Gale, she realised the foal was taking no notice of the halter swinging from her arm. Carefully, she slipped the rope round Gale's neck. Easy! The headpiece was far too big for the little foal, but she didn't seem to mind the rope round her neck at all. She followed Jenny around like a faithful puppy.

True to form, Midnight's curiosity got the better of him. He edged closer, seeking attention.

"You want to have a go, too, do you?" Jenny asked. She'd been planning this moment for days. She rubbed Midnight's neck with her hand until he relaxed. Then she rubbed his neck with the rope, and soon she managed to drop the end of the rope over his neck to form a loop – every movement slow and deliberate.

Now for the tricky part, Jenny thought, trying to sort out the headpiece with one hand while holding onto the neck rope with the other. Midnight turned his head to have a look at what she was doing, and pushed his nose straight into the nosepiece of the halter. Jenny couldn't believe her luck. Before he could have second thoughts, she quickly eased the remains of the halter over his ears. It was on!

Midnight snorted in alarm and shied, jerking his head away. Jenny grabbed hold of the rope around his neck, and the loose end whipped round, hitting his flank. He pulled back in earnest, bracing himself against the rope. Jenny hung on doggedly, but she was no match for the stallion. He reared up, fighting against the pressure round his head, and the rope jerked savagely from Jenny's hand. She caught a glimpse of his hooves and his wild eye, and then he galloped off with the long rope whipping around between his legs.

"*Ouch!*" wailed Jenny, nursing her hand. "Ouch! Ouch! Ouch!"

The mares and foals, alarmed by Midnight's sudden departure, galloped after the stallion in an excited flurry.

Jenny realised she now had a serious problem; her halter was still on Midnight, and she couldn't leave it there. She trudged after the ponies for what seemed like ages. As she'd feared, Midnight kept a safe distance from her. Several times he trod on the rope, but the halter stayed firmly on his head.

Jenny was so tired she couldn't think straight. The ponies had reached the main track, and the sun was setting. She decided to admit defeat and go home. As she turned to go, Midnight walked towards her, stopped at a marker stone and rubbed his head against it, working the halter loose over his ears. It flopped to the ground. He picked it up in his teeth, shook it fiercely and dropped it on the track a couple of yards from her, giving her a withering look as if to say, 'That's what I think of your stupid idea!' Then he walked away to join his mares.

The halter lay crumpled in the dust, inert and harmless. Jenny picked it up, and made her way home - mind numb, legs like jelly and dreams shattered.

CHAPTER EIGHT

"Sugar lumps," said Ben. "That's what you need. Horses like sugar lumps. I remember Grandpa saying that. He used to work with farm horses, you see. I remember him smothering a metal bit in treacle to get a young horse to accept it. After a while that horse shoved its head into the bridle, no problem. If you want Midnight to like the halter, he'll have to be given something nice while he's wearing it. Then he'll learn to like it."

"You're a genius!" Jenny exclaimed. "I can get sugar lumps from the Hotel; there are boxes of them in the kitchen." She hadn't dreamed the solution to her problem could be so simple.

If only she'd been able to talk to Ben sooner! She'd wasted precious time because it had been impossible to talk to him alone, with so many visitors on the island and so much work to do.

Now he'd found her playing the piano in the Tavern.

Ben pulled a chair next to Jenny. "Do you know any pop songs?" he asked. "How about *Here Comes Summer* by Cliff Richard?"

Jenny laughed. "Very appropriate!" she said, pointing at the gloomy rain outside. "It goes like this, doesn't it?"

They stayed in the Tavern all afternoon, playing songs and losing track of time.

The following day was a boat day. As usual, Jenny helped in the Hotel kitchen at lunch time and in the Tea Garden in the afternoon. This gave her plenty of opportunity to steal sugar lumps. She wore some baggy shorts, and filled the large pockets as much as she could without looking obviously lumpy. Stealing was easy because everyone trusted each other, and that made her feel even more terrible about it.

By the time she got home, some of the sugar lumps had worn away to a sticky dust in her pockets. She carefully salvaged what she could and transferred them into a paper bag. Then she changed, washed her shorts, hung them to dry, picked up the halter and went to find Midnight.

The ponies were loafing around on the west side, making the most of the evening sunshine and a slight south-westerly breeze which kept the flies at bay. They looked sleek, fat and content.

Trying to stay calm, Jenny hid the halter behind a rock and walked slowly towards the herd. As usual, it wasn't Midnight who came up first, but Gale. Jenny stroked her and offered her a sugar lump. The little foal sniffed it, explored it delicately with her lips and then nibbled it tentatively. Soon she was munching happily, and looking around for more.

Jenny laughed with delight. "You like sweeties, do you?" she asked, fondling Gale's soft, stumpy mane.

Midnight couldn't resist investigating what his daughter was eating with such obvious enjoyment. He snuffled at the bag, and drew back suspiciously when it rustled.

Jenny put a sugar lump on the palm of her hand and held it flat, remembering a photo in one of her pony books with the caption, 'The correct way to offer a titbit'.

Like Gale, Midnight investigated the sugar lump with his lips, and then took it between his teeth. *Crunch!* Eagerly he searched for more in the bag, and pinned his ears back at Gale when she tried to do likewise.

"Not so fast, Sunshine!" Jenny said. "You've got to earn your treats." She went to pick up the halter, and Midnight followed close behind. Carefully she put a sugar lump on her palm, and placed the nose loop of the halter above it so he'd have to push his nose through it to get his reward. It worked perfectly, followed by another lump when she slipped the halter over his ears. He snorted when he felt the rope tighten over his head, and started to pull back, but Jenny was ready with yet another sugar lump.

Jenny put the bag in her left hand, held the rope in her right hand and walked forwards. For an awful moment, Midnight hesitated. The rope went tight, and he pulled backwards. Quickly, Jenny offered a sugar lump a few inches in front of his nose, and he walked towards her instead.

After a few minutes of leading round in circles, there were only two sugar lumps left. Jenny gave them as a final reward once she'd eased the halter off.

Crunch! Crunch! Crunch! Sticky saliva dribbled down Midnight's lips. He raised his head and curled his top lip, savouring the intense taste of pure sugar.

Jenny ran across Ackland's Moor, laughing and leaping. Ben's idea had worked brilliantly! She couldn't wait to tell him. Midnight liked her again! Why hadn't she thought of sugar lumps before? They made horse-training so easy!

"We seem to be using a lot of sugar lumps this summer," Sheila remarked. She was making scone mixture, while Jenny rolled the dough, cut out rounds and placed them in neat rows on a tray, ready for baking.

"Oh?" Jenny's heart lurched.

"I think sometimes people take them to eat later, like

sweets. You can't trust anyone nowadays."

Jenny kept quiet.

"I've ordered another lot, so I just hope they arrive tomorrow. It'll be a job to use a whole crate by the end of the season now, but we'll have to try. It encourages the rats if there's too much food stored during the winter."

"I'm sure we'll use them up," Jenny said truthfully, and her mind wandered to Midnight.

Her training sessions were going quite well. Midnight now whinnied when he saw her, and he usually hurried over to her, eager to get some sugar – almost too eager. A worrying development was that he'd started approaching visitors, presumably to see whether they also carried sugar lumps. Some had even reported he'd 'attacked' them. Jenny was sure he hadn't actually attacked anyone, but it wasn't doing his reputation any good.

All this made it even more important for her to master riding him.

Jenny had a vision of riding Midnight down the High Street to the Tavern, with everyone looking on, speechless with admiration, or perhaps clapping – she hadn't quite decided which she preferred. Mr Bonham would be standing at the door to the Tavern, smiling in that special way. Midnight would halt in front of him, like a show pony in front of the judge.

"I can see that pony means the world to you, Jenny," he would say. "He can't possibly be shipped to the mainland now that you've tamed him. I'd like to give him to you, as a thank you for all the wonderful scones you've made. Just one thing, though, I'm afraid you won't be able to go to school, because Midnight will pine away without you."

"Oh, thank you, Mr Bonham," she'd say, and she'd dismount and shake his hand – or perhaps he'd kiss her lightly on the cheek, like grown-ups did.

That was her dream. The reality was that riding wasn't going at all well. She just couldn't seem to get Midnight to understand what she wanted, no matter how much she squeezed with her legs or pulled on the halter rope. It just ended up with him getting annoyed, and her getting frustrated to the point of despair. What she needed was someone to lead Midnight while she rode him. She decided to ask Ben to help her.

"Well, that's me done," Sheila said. She put a smooth, rounded mound of dough dusted with flour onto Jenny's marble slab. "Soft as a baby's bottom," she said, patting the dough with affection, and set about tidying up the kitchen with habitual efficiency.

Jenny swapped the scones around in the oven to make way for the final tray. Even though she'd been in the kitchen for a couple of hours, the smell of the scones as they came out of the oven still made her mouth water.

"Take a few scones home for your father," Sheila said, blushing through her freckles. "And for you, too, of course. Here, you'd better have some cream and jam to go with them."

Sheila's food parcels were becoming a fairly regular feature at Number One Barton Cottages, and Jenny never turned them down. Dad was good at lots of things, but cooking wasn't one of them.

Perhaps Sheila's taken pity on me because I'm so skinny, Jenny thought, clutching her box of goodies as she walked home.

That evening Jenny and Ben went to find Midnight. Jenny had lots of sugar lumps from her emergency store in her bedroom. Knowing they were in short supply made her feel doubly guilty about hoarding so many – nearly three boxes in all.

It was a damp, overcast evening. Midnight and some of the mares and foals were at the northern entrance to the quarries, near Halfway Wall. Nobody was about. Ideal.

"Shall I give you a leg-up?" Ben asked.

"I don't know. I usually just get on from a rock or broken-down wall."

"It's really easy. Just stand facing him and lift your left leg so I can hold your ankle – yes, like that – then we go one, two, three, hup!"

Jenny felt herself rise into the air with tremendous force. She nearly sailed right over Midnight's back, but grabbed hold of a handful of mane and somehow managed to land on top of him. She could tell he wasn't at all happy. "I think I'd better get down," she said nervously.

Ben smiled up at her, holding the halter rope loosely across the palm of his hand. "Nonsense! You'll be fine! I've got hold of him, look."

Everything happened very fast after that. There was a whinny from Middle Park, on the other side of Halfway Wall. Midnight's head shot up, and he whinnied back. Jenny felt him quivering. He broke away from Ben's loose hold, and started trotting purposefully towards the wall. It was jerky and uncomfortable, and Jenny clung onto his mane with all her strength as she wobbled around on his slippery back.

"Hey! Come back! Whoa! Slow down!" Ben yelled, running behind them.

"Shut up, Ben! You're not helping!" Jenny shouted.

"What? I can't hear you!" Ben's voice was further away now. "Oh, cripes! Hang on, Jenny!"

Midnight's pace quickened, and became smoother. Jenny could see his shoulders working like pistons below her. She felt his muscles bunch and stretch, creating raw, uncontrollable power.

A solid grey line loomed ahead, blurred through Jenny's watering eyes. A wall, she thought hopelessly. Halfway Wall! He must stop! *He must!*

The grey line became large, dark and unavoidable. She could just make out the outline of the slate stile by the Logan Stone. At least if they jumped the stile it wouldn't be quite so high, but if Midnight swerved to the right at the last minute they could both end up over the cliffs.

Midnight's ears pricked forward and he accelerated, full of confidence.

I'm going to die, Jenny thought. She felt remarkably calm about it - resigned to her fate.

Midnight's neck stretched out, and she felt a tremendous surge beneath her. They flew through the air, held together by two handfuls of mane. The blotchy granite wall flashed

beneath them, and then they started falling back down again. Jenny closed her eyes, and waited for the end.

Midnight landed with a jolt, jerking Jenny forward over his neck, and then back again, so she sprawled over his back as he galloped on without a pause. Her muscles screamed with the effort of hanging on, and she could taste blood in her mouth, but she was still on-board.

A bunch of mares and foals came galloping up to meet them, and Midnight slowed to a high-stepping, jarring trot, which was much more scary and uncomfortable than his gallop.

All Jenny's strength had gone. She felt like a rag doll. She'd have to let go. Hitting the ground would hurt, but at least that would be the end of it.

Midnight's head dropped abruptly. He stopped. Jenny lay halfway up his neck, knowing she'd gone beyond the point of no return. She slid off in slow motion and lay, rather dazed, in a large clump of heather.

He stood with his neck arched downwards, trying in vain to pull his head up. He'd trodden on the trailing rope of the halter with a hind hoof, and it was pinning his head to the ground.

As quickly as she could, Jenny worked at the halter until it was loose enough to slip over Midnight's ears, then she took it off.

He shook his head, and stood still for a moment, looking at her. Then he trotted away jauntily to his break-away herd.

Jenny sat on the prickly heather, relishing the fact it didn't move. She'd never felt such a mixture of emotions: terror, relief, pain, joy, exasperation and exhilaration all rolled into one. I've galloped on Midnight! I've jumped on Midnight! Oh, it was amazing! Never again, though, she thought. Never, *ever*, again!

"Jenny! Jenny! Are you all right? I'm so sorry!" Ben ran up, gasping and red in the face.

"Battered, bruised, but no broken bones." Jenny's voice echoed in her throbbing head. "It wasn't your fault. He'd have run off anyway, to get to the ponies."

"Yes, it *is* my fault!"

"What?"

"You see, I fetched some rubbish from Tibbett's with the tractor this afternoon, and I must have left the gate open. That's how some of the ponies ended up in Middle Park. The gate's still open. I'm so sorry!"

Jenny looked at Ben's red face staring down at her, and burst out laughing. She lay on the heather and laughed helplessly, so her aching sides ached even more. "Don't – worry! I – had – the – ride – of – my – life!" she managed to say. "He's – like – Pegasus! We – flew!"

With a sigh of relief, Ben plonked himself down on the ground beside Jenny, and started laughing, too.

They laughed so much that tears streamed down their faces. Eventually they lay exhausted, staring up at the grey sky. A thin drizzle drifted by on the breeze.

"I suppose we'd better get those ponies back where they belong," said Jenny. She felt so incredibly weak that even talking was an effort. "You won't tell anybody about this, will you?"

"No, of course not." Ben jumped up, and held out his hand.

Jenny took it, and he pulled her up. As she fell towards him, he gave her a quick hug. "I'm so glad you're okay," he said.

They parted, slightly embarrassed, and went to put the ponies back where they belonged.

CHAPTER NINE

The rest of the summer whizzed by. The weather was good, so Lundy was heaving with visitors. Work got in the way constantly, and left very little spare time for Jenny to spend with Midnight or Ben.

All too soon, it was Ben's last day on the island.

Jenny knew she would miss him terribly. There would be no possibility of meeting him somewhere by chance, or going swimming before breakfast – or anytime, come to that – and there would be nobody to help her with Midnight and share in her triumphs and disasters. Lundy would be a lonely place without Ben.

It was a mark of how much everyone liked Ben that they organised a leaving party for him. They'd all miss his easy smile and affable nature. He was a good worker, and didn't mind what he did. He fitted in.

The leaving party followed the familiar and well-loved pattern of parties in the Tavern, with food, drink and plenty of home-made entertainment.

As everyone finished their plates of food, Mr Hamilton got up and rapped the table for silence.

"Watch out! Speech-time!" Jenny whispered to Ben.

Ben made a face.

Mr Hamilton smiled at his audience. He thoroughly

enjoyed making speeches. "A few months ago, Albert approached me to enquire about a summer job for young Ben here. I considered..."

"That damned stallion! He tried to kill me, I swear it!" Gareth burst into the Tavern, stopping Mr Hamilton in mid-sentence. "I was walking along, minding my own business, and he came at me out of the blue! Galloping straight at me, he was! Scared me to death! He ought to be shot!"

Mr Hamilton's speech was forgotten. A crowd gathered round Gareth, eager to hear more.

Jenny's happiness evaporated. The room suddenly felt horribly crowded. She had to get out. "I'm sorry, Ben. I've got to go. I need some fresh air," she shouted in his ear. "Have a good time. I'll see you tomorrow."

The night was clear and bathed in silvery moonlight – like the night of Jenny's birthday, but not so warm. The air felt thinner, and tasted of autumn. Jenny gulped it in, like a drowning fish. The fun of the party seemed a distant memory. Midnight was in serious trouble, and she didn't know what to do.

"Everything's gone wrong!" she wailed to the starlit sky as she hurried up the High Street and past her cottage.

She heard footsteps running up behind her. "I'm so sorry, Jenny! It's my fault, isn't it? I was the one who suggested giving him sugar lumps, and now he chases after people, hoping they've got some. It must be that, mustn't it?" Ben caught up with her, and took hold of her arm. "Where are you going?"

"I'm going to see Midnight."

"But – oh, all right. I'll come with you."

"You can't. You'll miss your party."

"My party's finished. It seems to be Gareth's party now."

They walked on in companionable silence, disturbing

scores of sheep resting on the path. Their shoes squashed sheep droppings between the crunchy granite gravel underfoot. A strong, musty smell of sheep hung in the still, damp air.

As they approached Pondsbury, they heard the dull thud of hooves. Midnight came cantering towards them, leaping over the tussocks of gorse and heather in his way, and kicking up sprays of silvery dew-drops. He looked like a mythical creature in the moonlight.

"Oh, he's so beautiful!" Jenny whispered. "A storybook horse."

"Fairy tale, or horror story?"

Jenny sighed. "That's the trouble – he's a bit of both, isn't he?"

"Perhaps we should rename him Nightmare," Ben said.

"Oh! That's unfair! Poor Midnight!"

The stallion trotted up, ears pricked, eager for a treat. He nuzzled at Jenny's pockets.

"Sorry, old boy. No more sugar from now on. You're getting spoilt," Jenny said, pushing him away firmly as he tried to nip her pocket.

He turned to Ben, hoping for better luck, but Ben pushed him away, too.

Put out, Midnight turned away and stood with his ears back, swishing his tail sulkily.

Jenny walked round to his head, and started rubbing his neck and talking to him.

Midnight blew gently through his nose and rested a hind leg. His head lowered, his eyelids drooped and his lips trembled.

Jenny smiled to herself. "There! You see? This is much better than sugar, isn't it?" she said softly. "You're not to go chasing people again. They don't know you're just looking for food; they think you're attacking them. You can come up to me, but no one else. Understand? Now I'd better go, because it's Ben's last night."

Ben walked up to join her at Midnight's side. "It's OK, I'm quite happy stargazing," he said.

"Do you know what they're all called?" Jenny asked, looking up at the sky.

"Not all of them, but I know some. Dad taught me. Look, I'll show you." Ben stood behind Jenny, and pointed northwards over her shoulder. Jenny could feel the warmth of his body against her back.

"See those seven bright stars in the shape of a saucepan? That's the Plough, a part of Ursa Major, or the Great Bear."

"Oh, yes!" Jenny exclaimed.

"Now then," Ben continued, tracing a line in the sky with his finger while holding her hand in his. "Go on in a straight line from the lip of the saucepan, and you'll see the North Star, Polaris - it's the bright one, there. That's attached to a smaller saucepan, which is Ursa Minor, the Little Bear."

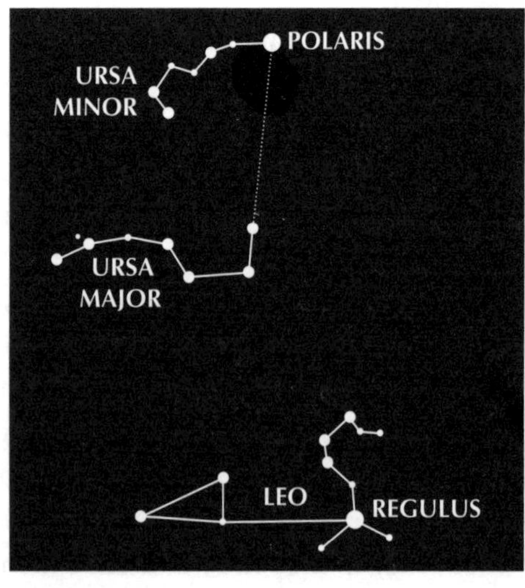

It's all so clear, once it's pointed out, Jenny thought. I must try to remember all this.

"Now then, if you pretend the big saucepan, Ursa Major, has a hole, and its contents have spilt out of the bottom of the pan, that's Leo. See? It's supposed to look like a lion."

"That's my star sign!" Jenny said.

"Well, there you are, then. You now know how to find your own stars."

"That star in the middle is much brighter than the rest, isn't it, Ben?"

"Yes, that's Regulus, the lion's heart."

Midnight stood with his head over Jenny's left shoulder. He seemed to be looking at the stars, too.

"When I'm away on the mainland, Midnight, you can look at that star and think of me, and I'll look at that star and think of you," Jenny said. She turned to stroke the stallion's neck, and looked eastwards to the distant dark strip of land beyond the sea, dotted with pin-prick lights.

At that moment, the mainland seemed as far away as the stars. Jenny wished it could stay that way forever.

Jenny stood at the Ugly, squinting into the distance as the boat, with Ben on board, disappeared from view. It was mid-afternoon, and she didn't know what to do. Normally she'd have been down on the beach, swimming and climbing rocks, or trying to hitch a ride with one of the fishermen. Now nothing seemed worth doing. She ached with loneliness, but couldn't bear the thought of company.

There's one more week to go, then I'll be leaving for the mainland, too, Jenny thought miserably. The previously distant dread of school suddenly seemed very real and unavoidable – like heading for a wall on a galloping horse.

The sound of children's voices, quick and piercing, interrupted her gloomy thoughts. Camilla appeared, hotly followed by William.

"Have you seen Hector?" Camilla lisped through her gappy teeth. "We're playing hide and seek, but we can't find him *anywhere!*"

"Looks like he's won, then," Jenny said.

"Do you want to play?" Camilla asked hopefully.

"Thanks, but I've got to go and cook Dad's supper," Jenny lied. Well, it was much kinder than saying she just wanted to be left alone – a white lie, she thought fleetingly.

Camilla looked crestfallen.

Jenny felt guilty. She liked Camilla a lot, and Hector was always playing mean tricks on her. He never played by the rules. "Tell you what," she said, "I'll look for Hector on my way home, and if I find him I'll tell him you found me instead, so you've won anyway."

"Thanks, Jenny! Come on, Will, tea time!" Camilla said, taking her brother's hand.

Their feet thudded away down the path to Millcombe.

Jenny walked slowly towards the village, through dapples of light and shade cast onto the ground through the leafy branches overhead. She couldn't face going home yet – couldn't face having to talk to anyone – so she veered right and took the path along the East Sidelands. The mainland was a solid blue-grey strip on the skyline, and the sea shimmered deep blue in the early evening sunshine. Ben would be on the home stretch by now, if he still thought of it as home. He'd told her last night that he'd never felt so much at home as he had on Lundy.

"I've always felt a bit like a square peg in a round hole, but somehow I seem to fit here," he'd said. "All the things I'm good at – practical stuff, like farming and fishing – are valued on Lundy. You're so lucky to live here."

Jenny knew she should feel lucky as she walked along staring blankly at the glorious view, but she just felt depressed. As she climbed up the hill towards the ruins of Quarter Wall Cottages, it occurred to her that she wasn't exactly keeping her promise to look for Hector. At that moment she heard a high-pitched cry. It sounded like someone shouting, "Help!" but it was probably just a gull; they could sound awfully human sometimes.

"Help! Help!"

Jenny stood still and listened, trying to pinpoint the cries. There was nobody to be seen.

"Please! Help!"

Jenny ran towards the ruins.

"Help! Somebody!"

Although the voice was squeaky with panic, Jenny was almost sure it belonged to Hector. She reached the old cottages, and looked through a gaping hole which had once been a window.

"Midnight! What on earth are you doing?" Jenny couldn't help being amused by what she saw.

"He's cornered me," Hector squealed from behind Midnight's bulk. "He's trying to eat me!"

"Nonsense!" Jenny said in her best Mrs Hamilton-style voice. "Of course he doesn't want to eat you. He just wants you to be his friend, that's all." Then, as an afterthought, she added, "You're not hurt, are you?"

"Yes! I've grazed my knee."

Jenny felt like laughing. Compared with the injuries she thought he'd have, a grazed knee was slightly comic. "Hang on," she said, climbing into the ruin and navigating a course around Midnight. "Let's have a look."

Hector stood, back against the wall, eyes wide, face pale and streaked with tears. As Jenny approached, he flung himself at her and clasped his arms around her neck, hanging on with a vice-like grip. "Thank you! You've saved my life!" he cried. He felt damp, and smelt horrible.

"H-he t-took all my s-sweets!" Hector sobbed "G-gobbled the lot! I h-hate him!"

Jenny winced as his fingernails dug into the back of her neck. Summoning all her patience, she said, "Never mind. I'll buy you some more."

"Lots more?"

Jenny thought she heard a thudding sound, like quick footsteps. She glanced behind her, and saw Midnight leaving. "Okay, then. Lots more," she said.

An awful thought occurred to Jenny. She untangled herself from Hector's arms, held his shoulders and stared at him earnestly. "I'll buy you lots of sweets," she said, "on condition you forget this ever happened. Okay? Midnight didn't want to hurt you. He just likes sweets, that's all. You mustn't tell anyone about today, because if you do they'll send him away."

"Good," Hector said. "I *want* him to go away. Forever."

Resisting the overwhelming urge to hit him, Jenny said, "Then I won't buy you those sweets."

"Don't care. A few poxy sweets aren't worth it. What else will you give me?" Hector asked.

Jenny thought desperately. "I haven't got anything..."

"Liar!" Hector interrupted, his eyes shining with triumph. "You've got those stamps Daddy gave you! He and Mr Hamilton were talking about them. Mr Hamilton said they were worth lots of money. If you give them to me, I won't tell anyone about Midnight."

Jenny hesitated. "Promise?"

"Promise."

She sighed. "Okay. I'll give them to you tomorrow."

"No, we're going home tomorrow. I want them now."

Jenny didn't want Hector to see inside her cottage, with its mismatched furniture and untidy clutter. "Okay, if you go back to Millcombe, I'll bring them down to you."

"No, I'm coming with you. I don't trust you, and I don't trust that stallion," said Hector. His sweaty, sticky hand gripped Jenny's bare arm.

She flinched away, quietly fuming, and set off at a fast walk towards the village. Hector kept up infuriatingly well, saving enough breath to whine incessantly about his precious sweets. Jenny eventually told him to shut up, and they walked the rest of the way in hostile silence.

The smug superiority on Hector's face when he saw the state of her kitchen did nothing to improve Jenny's mood. She went to the kitchen sink to wash her hands, and was mortified to find it piled high with congealed washing-up.

"You need a cleaner," Hector said.

"And you need to mind your manners," Jenny snapped. She dried her hands on a dirty towel which smelt of sheep, and went into her bedroom to get the stamps. "Don't you dare come in!" she ordered, fetching the precious bright white envelope from its hiding place, and returning to the kitchen with it.

Hector grabbed the envelope, and pulled at the sheet of stamps inside.

"Careful! They're valuable, for goodness sake!" Jenny said. "Oh, and your hands are dirty! Look at the envelope!" The beautiful white envelope had sticky fingerprints all over it.

"You're in no position to lecture me about dirt!" Hector replied.

"Why! You stuck-up, snotty little..."

The front door opened, and Robert Medway walked in. He looked flabbergasted. "Er, Hector! What are you doing here? Er, I mean, how, um, er," His sentence petered out, and he became lost for words as his eyes darted from the children to the kitchen and back again. "Er, sorry about the mess. It isn't usually, um..."

"It's not messy at all – just homely," Hector said graciously. He raised the hand holding the envelope. "I lent Jenny a comic, and I was just getting it back. I'd better go now; my parents will be wondering where I've got to."

"Oh, right you are."

"Goodbye, Mr Medway. Thanks for the comic, Jenny." Hector smiled angelically, and left.

"Nice boy," Robert Medway said as he walked over to the kitchen sink to wash his hands. "I'm so glad you've become friends at last."

CHAPTER TEN

Nothing much happened for the next couple of days. The weather turned wet and foggy. Jenny had lessons with Mrs Hamilton in-between working in the Hotel. On Monday there was a day-trip of depressed-looking visitors. Curiously, Dobbin came over on the boat, and booked into the Hotel. He usually visited Lundy in October.

Dave Dobson, nicknamed Dobbin, was a sharp-witted little man whose life had always revolved around horses: the army, racing yards, hunt stables, farms - you name it, he'd done it. Now, in his fifties, he knew most of the tricks of the trade, and made a good living from a horse-dealing business near Appledore.

It was said that Dobbin could sort out even the most difficult horse. This reputation was enhanced by his official role as the mainland's chief Lundy pony agent, breaker, dealer and all-round expert.

Each autumn, a few weeks before the big horse sale at Barnstaple Market, he came to Lundy to help sort the ponies and transport the ones to be sold over to the mainland. He always kept the ponies destined for market at his stables for a couple of weeks before the sale, so he could halter-break them. A pony wearing a halter always got a better price.

In general, Dobbin managed to halter-break each Lundy

pony in a few hours, because they were typically even-tempered and easy to train. He'd just tie them to a strong post, go away for a cup of tea, and leave them to work out that if they pulled it hurt and if they didn't it was much more comfortable. Then he'd slap the pony with a sack until it gave up panicking and pulling against the rope. The pony would now appear halter-broken and handled at the sale. Job done.

Sometimes, a pony hurt itself so badly fighting against the rope that it died, or had to be put down.

"You can't win them all," Dobbin would say.

As Jenny walked home for lunch on Tuesday, she heard a lot of shouting and banging from the shippen yard. Something squealed. A pig? It sounded more forceful than a pig.

A shiver of dread ran through her; she hurried towards the yard, more certain with every step that her fears would be confirmed. They were.

Several men stood in a wide semi-circle around a plunging, terrified horse. They waved their arms and shouted a lot, trying to drive him forwards. The horse wrestled madly against a rope around his neck. Dobbin stood in front of him, holding the long tail of the rope, keeping up the pressure.

The horse braced against the rope, slithering and grunting in a surge of effort. Someone hit him on the rump, and he plunged forward.

Dobbin took up the slack.

Trapped between the men, the horse reared. His forefeet flailed the air as he climbed higher and higher, stood vertically for a moment, overbalanced, lost his footing and fell on to the hard, wet surface of the yard with a sickening thud.

"Midnight! Oh, no! Stop! Stop it!" Jenny screamed, climbing over the yard gate and running towards Dobbin. "Stop it! Let him go!"

"Keep away, child. You could get hurt."

"*He's* the one getting hurt! What are you trying to do? Let him go!"

Robert Medway came over. "That's enough, Jenny. I'm sorry. You weren't supposed to see this, but it's for his own good. Dobbin, er, Mr Dobson, knows what he's doing. We're just trying to get Midnight into a shed so we can get a head-collar on him and take him down to the boat. He's going to have a nice new home on the mainland."

"In a dog food tin," Jenny heard Daisy murmur too loudly.

Robert frowned at him. "You go home now, and I'll be along in a minute," he said to Jenny.

Midnight scrambled to his feet. Sweat dripped from his flanks, and his stiffened legs trembled with fear. Dark red blood oozed from a gash on his knee. His wide, wild eyes studied everyone intently, waiting for their next move, ready to fight again.

All of a sudden, Jenny knew how she could save him - or at least give him the chance to save himself. "No, I'm staying," she said. "Midnight knows me. I'll help."

"Jenny, I really don't see how you can help, and I don't want you getting hurt. Leave it to Mr Dobson. He's the expert."

Before anyone could stop her, Jenny went to Midnight, and started stroking him, talking softly all the time.

He flinched away from her to begin with, but soon relaxed enough for her to feel confident about trying the next stage of her plan.

"Can you let go of the rope, please?" she asked Dobbin. "And then, please stand back so you don't scare him."

Dobbin glowered at Jenny, but did as she asked.

She gathered up the rope and headed for the double doors of the shippen. Midnight followed obediently. Jenny could sense the admiring disbelief of the men, as well as Dobbin's humiliation.

"Hold hard! We were going to put him in the smaller shed," Dobbin said.

"Oh, but there's much more room in the shippen. He'll be much happier in there," Jenny said innocently.

"Okay, then. Put him in there. It makes no odds," Dobbin muttered.

After a moment's hesitation, Midnight followed Jenny into the shippen.

She slipped the rope over his neck. "It's up to you now," she whispered. "Good luck!" Then she left, and bolted the doors behind her.

The men burst into spontaneous applause. Dobbin joined in half-heartedly.

There was a crashing, scraping sound.

Everyone looked alarmed. Jenny tried not to smile.

Dobbin pulled back the rusty bolts, opened the top door and looked inside. He swore loudly, flung the bottom door open and ran inside.

More swear words.

They all piled into the shippen to see for themselves. The back wall had several stones missing, and Midnight had gone. They were just in time to catch a glimpse of him jumping from the ducks' pen into Tent Field. Then, with a flick of his tail, he disappeared from view.

Jenny had never seen her father so angry. He paced round the kitchen, shaking with rage and spluttering out words like an erupting volcano.

"You *idiot!* All that effort! We had him! At long last, we

had him! But *you* let him go! *Deliberately* let him go!" He paused for breath, trying to calm down. "It's all so clear now! That's what happened the last time, wasn't it? When the mare and foal were in there? You had Midnight in there as well, but he escaped, didn't he? You put him in there today hoping he'd escape again, didn't you? *Didn't you?*"

"Yes," Jenny whispered.

"You silly, selfish little girl! You didn't even *think* to ask *why* we were catching him, did you? Oh no! You just thought you'd take the law into your own hands!"

A chair fell over with a crash as he accidentally brushed against it, taking a great pile of old magazines with it. They scattered over the floor. Jenny noticed the book Albert had given her as a birthday present was amongst them. That's where it had got to! She'd read half of it at breakfast one day, and then she'd lost it, but it had been there all the time.

"And why the hell are you *smiling*, may I ask?" Robert shouted.

"That's my book. I thought I'd lost it," Jenny mumbled, her eyes fixed on the kitchen floor. Hector's right, she thought, we need a cleaner.

"Have you been listening to a word I've said?" Robert hissed. "*A book!* You're worrying about a damned *book!* This isn't some ridiculous pony story about wild stallions, gymkhanas and happily-ever-after rubbish, you know! This is *real life!*" Robert leant on the table, and spoke slowly and deliberately. "Real life is messy and complicated, and things never turn out as they should. Try this for a real life story: Midnight attacks Hector, and nearly kills him. Mr Bonham, understandably, wants Midnight destroyed. He asks me to do it. However, knowing you're fond of the brute, I ask if Midnight can be sent to the mainland instead. Mr Bonham very generously agrees, organises the boat and pays for Dobbin to come over. All goes well. The weather is good, we manage to catch Midnight, and it looks as if he'll be in a cosy stable on the mainland by nightfall. But then you come along.... And I think you can fill in the rest, can't you, Jenny?"

Jenny felt weak with the full realisation of what she'd done.

"So now," Robert said, "there isn't a hope in hell of catching him before the boat goes in an hour or two, and I'll have to go and shoot him later on, when everything's calmed down a bit. I'm sorry to be so brutal, Jenny, but that's the reality."

Jenny fled into her room and flung herself onto her bed, wailing in anguish, gulping for air, drowning in her own grief. Her agony for Midnight was mixed with rage against Hector. He'd broken his promise! He'd lied! How *could* he?

She sensed her father had come into the room.

"Jenny?" His voice wasn't angry any more, just sad. "I'm sorry, love. Truly I am. I didn't..."

"Go away! I hate you!" Jenny screamed.

A few minutes later, she heard him walk in and put something on the pile of clean clothes on top of her chest of drawers.

"Your book," he said softly.

She heard the book fall onto the floor with a thump.

Then she heard him washing up.

After a while, the noise from the kitchen changed. The radio crackled into life, and there were intermittent thumping, scraping and clattering noises. It sounded as if some serious cleaning was going on.

Jenny rolled over and sat up on the side of her bed, occasionally shuddering with yet another heart-wrenching sob. She longed for her father's strong, reassuring arms round her, but she couldn't face him. She was stuck in her room, and couldn't think what to do.

Absent-mindedly, she stared at the book on the floor. It had fallen face-down, open, with the spine bent back and the dust jacket half-off. It had a picture of a small boy standing on a very small planet surrounded by stars. The title, *The Little Prince*, was written across the top. The boy looked like a small version of Ben, complete with an untidy mop of fair hair. Jenny sighed and picked up the book. She took great pride in her books, and hated to see them damaged. As she turned it over to replace the dust jacket, an open page caught her eye. Stunned, she read and re-read it. A fox was asking the little prince to tame him, so they could become friends. The fox said that the little prince would have to be patient and quiet, and sit a little closer every day – just as Jenny had done with Midnight.

She read on, lapping up every word. The last thing the fox said took Jenny's breath away: "*Men have forgotten this truth,*" *said the fox.* "*But you must not forget it. You become responsible, forever, for what you have tamed....*"

"I can't let Midnight die!" Jenny said to herself. "I've tamed him, so I'm responsible for him. I've got to save him!"

She rummaged around in her drawer for the rope halter and the last box of sugar lumps.

Her anorak hung on the back of the door. Trying to make as little noise as possible, she put it on, filled the pockets with sugar lumps, opened her bedroom window and climbed out.

She sprinted up the track towards Quarter Wall, repeating under her breath, "Please let me find him in time! Please let everything be all right!"

CHAPTER ELEVEN

Somehow, Jenny knew the ponies would be down by the quarries. Her heart hammered in her chest when she saw them, but she forced herself to calm down. She knew Midnight wouldn't allow himself to be caught if she were nervous. This was her one-and-only chance to put things right. If she failed, Midnight would die – she was sure of that. Her father wouldn't lie about something so serious, and he was an excellent shot. He never missed a rabbit, and Midnight would be a much easier target than a rabbit. She shuddered at the thought.

Midnight stopped grazing and walked away as she approached him. For a moment she was terrified he'd run. She put the halter down, and took some sugar lumps out of her pocket.

He turned to face her – wary, but interested.

Jenny put a sugar lump in her mouth and sucked it, hoping it would lure him in. She ate a few more, realising she hadn't eaten anything since breakfast.

Midnight pawed the ground uncertainly, and kept his distance, but Gale came up. She'd grown into a stocky, rather scruffy little filly. A sandy-coloured winter coat grew unevenly between her creamy baby hair, and her legs were blotchy as they turned from light to dark.

"Hello, gorgeous. Want a sweetie?" Jenny said.

Gale crunched a sugar lump happily, and nudged Jenny for more.

Jenny stroked her and talked to her, and gave her an occasional titbit. Every second counted, but she had to pretend she had all the time in the world.

Eventually, Midnight walked up and pinned his ears back at Gale, warning her off. Then he pricked his ears forward, giving Jenny an innocent, pleading look.

From devil to angel in less than a second, Jenny thought. She gave him a sugar lump, and another, and another. His guard dropped, and he allowed her to slip the halter over his head while he munched. Then, feeding him sugar lumps at regular intervals, she led him along the track, past the Timekeeper's Hut, round the edge of Quarry Pond, up the hill and over to the Quarter Wall gate. The mares and foals followed at a respectful distance, with Rosie in the lead.

Midnight was concentrating so hard on the contents of Jenny's pockets that it was only when they had nearly reached Barton Cottages, and the mares gathered beyond the Quarter Wall had started calling, that he noticed he'd left the herd behind. Instantly agitated, he whinnied loudly and tried to rear.

Jenny fed him a handful of sugar lumps, and kept walking.

He tossed his head, hitting her head and spraying her with sugary froth from his mouth. Then he plunged forwards, squealing and whinnying in the same breath.

Jenny's head throbbed, and a searing pain burnt into her hands as the rope dragged through them, but she hung on and jerked with all her might on the rope. "Stop it! Behave!" she shouted. Her hands stung even more, and her eyes blurred with tears.

Midnight, obviously astonished, wheeled round and

stood still. He looked magnificent: ears pricked, eyes flashing, neck arched, tail high and every muscle in his body taut with anticipation. Ready to explode into action. Terrifying.

Jenny gave him yet another sugar lump. It had red blotches on it from her bleeding hand, but he didn't seem to notice. His sugary saliva stung her palm. Ignoring the pain, she reached inside her pocket for more sugar. There were only a couple of lumps left.

It's hopeless! I won't be able to get him to the yard, let alone down to the Landing Beach, she thought desperately.

Without warning Midnight spooked at something behind him. He wheeled round, knocking Jenny sideways. She knew she'd lose him for good if she fell over, so somehow she stayed upright and clung on to the rope.

"Jenny! What on *earth?* I thought you were in bed!"

"Careful, Dad! You frightened him. Keep back," Jenny said quickly. "I'm almost out of sugar lumps. Can you get some? They're under my pants."

"*What?*"

"Sugar lumps, in my bedroom. There's a box in the top drawer, under my pants." Jenny managed to sound much calmer than she felt. "Please hurry."

After what seemed like ages, her father came back with the box, and carefully gave it to Jenny.

"Thanks," she said, offering Midnight several in one go. "Somehow, I've got to keep his mind off the mares and get him down to the boat."

She expected her father to say she didn't have a chance, but he just said, "I'll walk behind, then, and we'll take it one step at a time."

All went well until they neared the Tavern, where Dobbin and his helpers had decided to pass the time until the tide was right for the boat to leave.

Daisy came out of the door. “Hell’s bells!” he exclaimed, and went back into the Tavern. “Come and look at this, you lot!” he bellowed.

Everyone crowded out of the Tavern, whistling, cheering and clapping.

Midnight stopped, petrified, eyes bulging. At any moment he’ll bolt, Jenny thought. She held the rope tightly, trying to ignore the stinging pain in her hands. The grand entry of her dreams, with Midnight perfectly under control, wasn’t turning out quite as she’d planned.

“Quiet!” Dobbin yelled above the din.

The noise subsided to an excited murmur.

“Right then,” Dobbin said, taking charge. “Just stay there for a moment, there’s a good girl. Don’t let go, now. I’ll get a proper headcollar and take over from here. You’ll never be able to hold him going down the Beach Road.”

Someone handed Dobbin his special headcollar, which had a chain running through it for extra control. He approached confidently, clicking his tongue softly against his teeth. “There’s a good boy,” he coaxed. His eyes narrowed in concentration and his body tensed, like a cat ready to pounce.

Midnight sensed it, and shied away, yanking the rope through Jenny’s raw hands.

She gasped with pain. “Please don’t! You’re upsetting him. I’ll manage.”

“Suddenly you’re the horse expert, are you?” Dobbin sneered. “Give him to me.” He grabbed hold of the rope.

Midnight struck out with a forefoot, hitting Dobbin’s leg so hard that he reeled backwards in agony.

“Why, you little beggar! Just you wait!” he hissed, nursing his leg and his wounded pride. His hard eyes focused on Jenny. “Okay, you take him, then. But don’t you dare let go!” He walked back to the crowd, trying to conceal a limp. "The pony's used to the girl, so it's best if she takes him," he said. "James and Daisy, walk in front with me. We'll stop him if he tries to makes a dash for it."

Jenny secretly doubted whether a hundred people would be able to stop Midnight if he made a dash for it.

"The rest of you, walk behind with Robert. Go steady, and don't get too close. That pony's got a kick like a mule."

Jenny offered Midnight a few sugar lumps, but he wasn't interested in them anymore; either he'd had enough or he was too upset. She walked forwards again, praying he'd follow.

She needn't have worried. He followed her willingly, wary of all the people around him, and seeking her protection. The lead rope hung loosely as he walked with his head near her shoulder, as if tied by an invisible thread. He wanted to be with her; he believed she would look after him; she had tamed him.

Silent tears trickled down her cheeks as she walked down the Beach Road to the waiting boat.

The sea looked oily-calm. At least the crossing won't be rough, thought Jenny.

"We'll take over now," Dobbin said once they reached the Landing Beach. He held a large canvas sling with a pole running through it. Several buckles and a rope attached to a ring hung from it, swinging and clanking.

Midnight pushed into Jenny, seeking reassurance.

"It's OK. They're not going to hurt you," Jenny soothed, stroking his neck. He knows I'm lying, she thought. Her hands shook.

"Hold this, Daisy. We'd better tie him first," said Dobbin, handing Daisy the sling so he could unravel a piece of rope which had been coiled over his shoulder. "James, come and take the lead rope. I don't want that child getting hurt."

James looked nervous as he walked up to take his place.

"It's okay, I'll be fine," Jenny said bravely. "I want to stay with him."

"This is no place for a girl. Let James have him now," Dobbin said firmly.

"No! He needs me!"

"Do as you're told! You've caused us enough trouble already," Dobbin barked.

"There's no need for that sort of talk. Come on Jenny, you've done your bit. I'll take you home," her father said kindly.

James took the rope from Jenny. She stroked Midnight's trembling neck. "Good luck," she whispered. Through a blur of tears she caught a glimpse of a blue eye, wide and frightened.

As she walked away, Midnight tried to follow.

"Oh, no you don't, you brute!" James said, jerking the lead rope.

"Hold him steady, James, and I'll tie him so he doesn't kick us while we put the sling on," she heard Dobbin say. Then she heard the crashing of shingle as Midnight tried to break free, and a thud as he fell over. Swearing and shouting from the men. Terrified, outraged grunting and squealing from Midnight. More crashing.

Jenny heard, but she dared not look.

Even if everything went according to plan, Jenny knew the journey ahead would be terrible for Midnight. With the sling secured round his stomach, he would be attached by a rope to a rowing boat with three men in it. Another rope would run from the rowing boat to the larger boat out in the bay. The men at the front would pull the rowing boat towards the larger boat, and the man at the back would hold onto Midnight's head to stop him from drowning. Then, on reaching the big boat, Midnight's sling would be attached to a system of ropes and pulleys on the boat, and he'd be winched into the hold. The hold was a small, stuffy place below the deck. If the boat made it to Bideford before Midnight wrecked it, he'd have to be winched ashore and transported by lorry to Dobbin's yard.

Jenny knew lots of ponies and cattle made the same tortuous journey from Lundy to the mainland every year – it was the only way to get them to market – but that wasn't any consolation.

I shouldn't have caught him, she thought miserably. He'd have been better off dead on Lundy, where he belongs.

She trudged up the Beach Road, grateful of her father's strong, protective arm around her shoulders. "What'll happen to him?" she asked after a while.

"He'll be fine, don't you worry. Mr Dobson will look after him and train him, and then he'll sell him on to a good home."

"Where will he sell him?"

"I don't know, Jenny love. The autumn horse sale in Barnstaple is where he usually sells the ponies."

"How can you be sure he'll go to a good home if he's going to be sold at market? He may go for, for d-dog f-food." Jenny stammered. The tears welled up again.

That night Jenny couldn't sleep. She put some jeans and a jumper on over her pyjamas, and climbed out of her bedroom window.

Stars sparkled in the ink-black sky.

Had Midnight arrived safely? She wouldn't know until Mr Hamilton made his morning radio call to the Hartland Coastguard. There was nothing she could do but wait. She searched the sky and found the Plough, then Leo the lion, and then Regulus, the lion's heart.

"I'm so sorry, Midnight," she said. "You trusted me, and I betrayed you. I don't know how yet, but I'm going to make everything all right when I get to the mainland. I won't let you down again, I promise."

CHAPTER TWELVE

The boat heaved through the lumpy waves and belched diesel fumes over the deck. Shivering uncontrollably, Jenny groaned, hung her head over the side and was sick yet again. In the brief period afterwards, when she felt well enough to think of anything other than survival, panic gripped her. In a few hours she'd be at St Anne's School for Girls. It was utterly impossible. She wanted to die.

All around, the dark metallic sea merged with heavy low clouds. Lundy, in one direction, and the North Devon coast, in the other, were somewhere behind the grey shroud, but she had no idea where. She was in a violent, liquid no-man's-land. The only indication that the boat was on course came from a strong south-westerly wind, which buffeted her and blew her hair in front of her face.

Bang! A wave smashed into the boat head-on, sending a cascade of spray into the air. The prow reared up and then dropped into the void left by the passing wave. *Crash!* The boat quivered, rose and plunged again, boring through endless troughs and peaks in the turbulent sea.

She gripped the side of the boat and retched on a cramped, empty stomach. It felt as if she were being turned inside-out.

Jenny glanced over at Mrs Hamilton. She didn't look well, either.

A strong hand rested briefly on her shoulder.

"Why don't you come into the cabin, Jenny? It's warmer in there," said Captain Dover.

She nodded in reply. Mrs Hamilton's advice that the deck was always the best place to be if you felt sick didn't seem right; a warm cabin sounded much better.

The boat teetered, fell and wallowed, heeled, swayed and rocked, but Captain Dover walked along the deck as if he were taking a stroll up the High Street. Jenny tried to follow as best she could, lurching shakily from one hand-hold to the next until she reached the sanctuary of the small cabin.

"Lie here, maid. It's always better if you lie down," said the Captain, pointing to a short wooden bench. "You can use this jersey as a cushion, if you like."

The jersey was chunky and rough. It smelt of stale tobacco, engine oil and fish, but Jenny was past caring. It was a shred of soft comfort in the hard, wet, cold world she'd been plunged into. She sank onto the bench and curled up on her side, with the jersey scrunched into a makeshift pillow under her head.

Lunging and creaking, the boat juddered on. Jenny braced herself as she was flung inwards, and then her back bumped against the cabin wall as she was flung outwards. Brace, bump, brace, bump, brace, bump - her body rocked to and fro as the waves rolled and crashed.

There was another man in the cabin. He seemed unbelievably relaxed. Captain Dover took over the helm, and the two men talked and joked. Their low voices rose and fell against the noise of the engine. Jenny closed her eyes. Perhaps, against all odds, she'd survive the journey. Perhaps she'd see Ben, and they'd rescue Midnight somehow. Perhaps school would be okay after all.

The men's voices faded into a distant corner of her mind.

Jenny woke with the certain knowledge she was going to be sick. She had that unmistakable tingling feeling as her mouth filled with saliva. Through her half-opened eyes she could see Captain Dover smoking a pipe with great enthusiasm, filling the cabin with thick, pungent smoke. The other man had left the cabin.

Before she could get up, Jenny was sick. She was sick on her hair and on the jersey she'd been using as a pillow. It was so embarrassing that for a brief moment she considered running out on deck and jumping overboard. Instead, she just sat there and stared in disbelief as the slimy bile seeped into the wool.

"I am *so* sorry," she whispered, not daring to look up.

"Ha! Don't you worry!" Captain Dover said heartily. "It's due for a wash. It's had worse things on it, I can tell you."

Jenny wondered what on earth could be worse than sick.

"Here, you'd better clean yourself up. We're coming into Bideford," Captain Dover said, handing her an oil-stained towel which didn't smell much cleaner than the jersey. "You're in good company," he added, winking.

Mrs Hamilton came into the cabin. She looked different – sort of blue and unusually ruffled, but also different in her face. Her mouth was pinched and wrinkled, and her speech was slurred.

Until then, Jenny had never thought of teeth as being important for anything other than eating. Mrs Hamilton must have lost her false teeth overboard when she was sick. How on earth could she take Jenny to school now? It would be *so* embarrassing!

Captain Dover handed a small box to Mrs Hamilton. "Put your dentures back in, Peggy. Here's Bideford." He turned to Jenny and said in a stage whisper, "She was queasy a few years back, and parted company with her gnashers, so now I keep them safe for her if we're in for a bumpy ride."

Usually Jenny would have laughed, but all she managed was a wan smile of relief. Through the misty cabin window she could see the solid grey outline of a large, unfamiliar coastline dotted with buildings. She felt panic tingling through her body and grabbing at her heart. The boat, which had seemed like hell on earth an hour ago, was now a safe haven. It was her link with Lundy. She didn't want to leave it and embark on the most daunting journey of her life: the journey to boarding school.

CHAPTER THIRTEEN

As soon as Jenny stepped off the boat onto Bideford Quay, she felt like an alien in a chaotic, overpopulated foreign country. The only comfort was that the inhabitants spoke the same language, more or less.

In contrast, Mrs Hamilton seemed excited and very much at home. A trip to the mainland for a couple of days was a rare treat, and it was clear she intended to enjoy every minute of it.

"Let's go to my hotel and get changed. Then we'll have a spot of lunch and take a taxi to St Anne's. How does that sound?"

Fine, except for the last bit, Jenny thought. "Fine," she said, making a brave attempt at a smile.

Jenny felt chilled to her core. She sank gratefully into the huge hotel bath. Even tepid water made her skin sting, but as she thawed out she topped up the bath with more hot, clear water from the impressive brass mixer tap which gurgled and gushed when turned on. Soon the bath was full to the overflow pipe.

The water on Lundy was always peaty-brown and in short supply. This was luxury.

The hotel soap smelt like a summer garden. She washed her body and her hair, and then allowed herself several minutes of pure indulgence – not thinking, just feeling. She drifted about, soaking in warmth, blocking out all thoughts of what was to come...

Knock! Knock! "Jenny? Are you all right in there?" Mrs Hamilton's voice made her jump.

She scrambled out of the bath, spilling water onto the bathmat and surrounding floor. "Yes, thanks! Coming!"

The bath towels were white, thick and soft. Jenny wrapped one round her, and tried to empty the bath. After several futile attempts at pulling out a shiny metal disc, which appeared to be the bath plug, she managed to make it pop up by pulling a lever below the tap. Fascinating! She did it several times, for fun.

"Jenny?"

"Just coming!"

"So is Christmas."

Reluctantly, Jenny emerged from the steaming bathroom: bright red, squeaky clean and cocooned in a massive towel.

"How very apt!" Mrs Hamilton exclaimed, smiling. "You look like a chrysalis, ready to transform into a butterfly! I've hung your school uniform on the back of the door, and there's a hairdryer over there on the dressing table. You get ready, while I have a quick bath." She disappeared into the bathroom, and shut the door.

Jenny heard the gurgle and gush of the bath tap. Gingerly, she took down her uniform and put it on, piece by uncomfortable piece.

The starched white shirt felt crisply cold against her warm body.

The long navy blue woollen socks were itchy and too big. They kept trying to fall down.

Likewise, the pleated blue tartan kilt-skirt was too big in all directions. It hung loosely on her hips, rather than at her waist, so that the hem nearly reached her ankles.

At least the blazer hid everything else. It dwarfed her, hanging shapelessly from her narrow shoulders and finishing just below her bottom.

I must have lost a lot of weight, Jenny thought, despairing at her image in the mirror - probably several pounds during that boat trip alone. She put her blue-and-grey-striped tie round her neck, pushed it under the stiff shirt collar and attempted to tie it. The harder she tried, the worse it turned out. She had another go, and another.

Mrs Hamilton emerged from the bathroom, dressed in a tweed skirt, twin-set and pearls. "Well, what a transformation! You do look smart!"

Jenny rounded on her, courageous in her despair. "No I don't! It's all far too big! Hideous! I can't have shrunk *that* much since you measured me in the summer!"

Unphased, Mrs Hamilton said, "I ordered a size larger, to give room for growth. Girls your age do grow tremendously quickly; you wait and see. Come here, and I'll show you how to tie your tie."

Jenny found Mrs Hamilton's ability to ward off rebellion infuriating, but rather reassuring at the same time.

As Mrs Hamilton deftly placed the tie around Jenny's neck, the familiar smell of her scented talcum powder wafted in the air. "This is by far the easiest method, and quite adequate for school," she said. "Mr Hamilton would be appalled, of course; he likes a Windsor knot, but that's rather more complicated. He always says you can tell a gentleman by the way he knots his tie. Now then, we'll call the longer, fatter end A, and the shorter, thinner end B, shall we?"

Without pausing for a reply, Mrs Hamilton continued, "Cross A over B, then turn A back underneath B, and back over the front of B again. Then pull A up and through the back of the loop around your neck, hold the front of the knot loosely with your index finger and bring A down through the front loop of the tie, remove your finger and tighten the knot snugly, like so. There! Bob's your uncle. Now you try."

After several attempts, Jenny mastered it, and wondered why she'd found it so difficult.

"Jolly good! That's that, then. You do look smart! Shoes on. Time for lunch," said Mrs Hamilton.

The shoes were shiny, stiff and at least a size too big. They made a flapping noise as Jenny walked cautiously down the stairs.

She felt light-headed with hunger at the intense smell of hot food which greeted them as they walked into the plush, stuffy dining room. The tables had spotless white linen tablecloths. They were laid with stiff white linen table napkins folded into fans, a spectacular array of silver cutlery, and sparkling glasses of various shapes and sizes. The chairs had ornate frames and deep purple upholstery. Jenny felt out-of-place as she followed Mrs Hamilton to their table - weaving between some seated diners - with her eyes fixed on the carpet to avoid looking at anyone. The carpet was also deep purple, with elaborate gold swirls which made her rather dizzy.

A waiter held out her chair and called her 'young lady'. The hot, airless room began to turn, leaving her behind. This is all a weird dream; I'll wake up on Lundy in a minute, she thought....

"Mum?" Jenny murmured. "Mummy, is that you?" Through a haze of semi-consciousness she saw the most beautiful face looking tenderly at her, and felt her hand being stroked gently. I must have died and gone to heaven, she thought.

"No, dear. I'm not your mother. You fainted, but you'll

be fine. Lie still for a minute or two, and then we'll get you onto a chair. Your mother's just here."

"I'm afraid her mother is no longer with us. I'm her guardian," said Mrs Hamilton.

"Oh, I'm so sorry. I didn't realise."

Fully conscious now, Jenny was overwhelmed with embarrassment. She lay on the swirly carpet, surrounded by cutlery, broken glass and table linen, and stared in dismay at the concerned faces looking down at her: Mrs Hamilton, the waiter, a bald man with tortoiseshell-framed glasses, a slim girl with short, dark hair and almost identical glasses, and the beautiful lady – now clearly not her mother.

"Oh, I'm so sorry! I-I didn't mean, I mean, oh dear!" Tears stung Jenny's eyes. I mustn't cry! I *mustn't!* She thought, closing her eyes tightly.

"It's my fault entirely – so stupid of me," she heard Mrs Hamilton saying. "We've just come over from Lundy, you see, and Jenny was terribly ill on the boat. She hasn't had anything to eat since six o'clock this morning, poor thing."

"Would my Coca Cola help? I haven't drunk from it," said the girl.

She sounded nice, and so did the suggestion of a Coke. Jenny felt parched, with a peculiar metallic taste in her mouth. She opened her eyes and smiled at the girl crouched by her side, holding a glass of cool, sweet Coke.

The girl smiled back. She had a brace over her teeth, and spoke with a slight lisp. "Hello. I'm Frances," she said. "Are you starting at St Anne's, too?"

Frances' parents introduced themselves as John and Jessica Knighton.

"My goodness! Aren't you our new MP?" Mrs Hamilton exclaimed.

"I'm afraid so," Mr Knighton replied, smiling. He asked

Mrs Hamilton and Jenny to join his family for lunch, and offered them a lift to St Anne's afterwards.

By the time they were ready to leave the hotel, Mrs Hamilton had told John Knighton exactly what she'd do if she were Prime Minister. Jenny and Frances had discovered they were the two new girls who had been awarded scholarships. Furthermore, they both played the piano, loved singing and hoped to be picked for the school choir. In many ways, though, they were complete opposites. Frances had been born and raised in London where, it seemed, every minute of her time had been filled with organised activities like dance, drama, music and extra coaching for the scholarship exam. Her idea of fun was a trip to a museum or the theatre. She'd never been near a pony, and she didn't want riding lessons.

Oh well, Jenny thought as she settled into the beige leather seats of the Knightons' black Bentley, at least I've made one friend. I'm bound to find some girls who like horses, and I'll make friends with them, too. Perhaps I'll end up with lots of friends!

The car purred down the road. Jenny felt like royalty as they passed along the bustling quayside.

A familiar figure puffed on his pipe and talked to some men mending lobster pots. They all looked up at the Bentley as it passed.

"Coo-ee! Captain Dover!" Jenny shouted, rubbing at the misty window and waving frantically.

He took his pipe out of his mouth, smiled and held his hand up in a brief greeting before turning back to his friends.

"Jenny! Behave yourself!" Mrs Hamilton scolded.

For the first time Jenny felt completely trapped in her new, strange life – like a goldfish in a bowl, looking out at the real world. She longed to be with the fishermen on the quay.

The car turned smoothly over the bridge and then accelerated along a broad road. Jenny flinched every time traffic passed in the opposite direction, expecting a crash. She wasn't used to cars.

Unfamiliar trees, hedges and fields whizzed by. The adults chatted politely, but the two girls fell silent.

St Anne's School for Girls stood, solid and imposing, at the top of a long drive flanked by parkland. Huge trees dotted the lush pasture, which was enclosed by wrought iron fencing. Jenny looked out for ponies, but all she could see were brown cattle and a few sheep.

The two fields nearest the house had goal nets in them.

"Oh, no! Lax pitches!" Frances groaned.

"What's lax?" Jenny asked.

"Lacrosse. A terrible form of torture invented by sadistic games teachers."

"Actually, it was invented by the Native Americans. They called it the Creator's Game, and it was often used to solve disputes between tribes," Mrs Hamilton said, slipping effortlessly into schoolteacher mode. "It's a great game. I used to love it when I was a girl; I was even team captain for a couple of years. Being in a team is such a good way to make friends, I always think."

They parked next to a row of cars, all shiny and expensive-looking.

Several confident, well-dressed parents stood talking while their immaculate daughters chatted and laughed together. Other families greeted each other as they carried suitcases, trunks and lacrosse sticks in various directions with the certainty of soldier ants.

Jenny studied the daunting scene from the sanctuary of the Bentley. The new girls are supposed to arrive a day before everyone else, but everyone here seems to know each other already, she thought. Everyone seems to know what to do and where to go. They don't seem 'new' at all. This is much worse than I'd imagined!

Mrs Hamilton turned round in her front seat, and beamed at Jenny and Frances. "Here we are, girls! Isn't this exciting?"

CHAPTER FOURTEEN

The noise was the worst thing, Jenny decided after a few days at St Anne's. Worse than having every minute of your day organised, and worse than having to hide in the loo for a few moments of solitude.

The day started with First Bell at a quarter-to-seven. This woke Jenny with the ferocity of a hurricane, smashing through precious dreams of home or blissful, oblivious sleep. Second Bell followed five minutes later, just as Jenny's heart rate was approaching normal again. Everyone then had twenty minutes to wash in freezing-cold water, queue for the loo, get dressed, make beds and tidy up before Breakfast Bell rang. That was just the beginning. The whole day was governed by bells for lessons, breaks, meals, games sessions and even Last Bell for lights-out. Between the bells, noise was supplied by people chattering, talking, shouting, scolding, lecturing, laughing and screaming. The noise didn't even stop after dark. Jenny's dormitory – 'dorm' in school language – had nine other girls in it, and they all talked for ages after lights-out. Susie, the Dorm Prefect, was supposed to stop them, but she was the worst offender with her incessant talk about boys.

Jenny took to sleeping with tissues stuffed in her ears.

As she'd thought, most of the new girls already knew each other. They'd moved on to St Anne's together from a school called Norwood House, and they guarded their friendships jealously. Within a few days the Third Form had developed an insecure pecking order, with the popular set at the top and assorted misfits at the bottom. Anyone trying to work their way up was very careful to avoid contact with people obviously less popular than themselves, for fear of demotion.

This system, with its merciless unwritten rules and rituals, seemed totally normal to the other girls. Jenny couldn't understand it at all. It seemed that skill at games, good looks and loud self-confidence earned lots of popularity points. Academic ability, shyness and physical imperfections sent you plummeting down the league table. Being a nice person didn't count at all.

Jenny and Frances were labelled swots for winning the scholarships, and found themselves at the bottom of the pile, along with spotty Alison, shy Pandora, asthmatic Dorothy, nervous Jane and fat Belinda. They became an unlikely group of friends, united in adversity. Frances soon became known as Fran, and some other girls acquired less flattering nicknames. Jenny was glad nobody gave her a nickname. She'd always been Jenny – as in Jenny's Cove.

To Jenny's disappointment, none of her new friends liked riding. It appeared to be a hobby exclusively enjoyed by popular girls, who talked enthusiastically about riding, the Pony Club, competitions and anything to do with horses and ponies. Jenny hovered round them, like a moth attracted to a light, drawn by the conversation and longing to join in.

It was during one of her eavesdropping sessions that she discovered there would be no riding lessons until after half term, because the horses at Home Farm Equestrian

Centre had equine influenza. Some of the girls had horses stabled there during term time, so they were especially worried.

Dejected, Jenny walked away. She hadn't realised horses could get flu. Her twin goals of learning to ride and rescuing Midnight seemed further away than ever. She had no idea how she would *find* Midnight, let alone get him a good home! Her best bet was to make friends with some of the horsey girls – but how?

Mrs Hamilton's no-nonsense voice popped into her head: 'Being in a team is such a good way to make friends, I always think'.

Lacrosse – known as 'lax' – was becoming Jenny's favourite sport, mainly because of where it was played. The lax pitches had tremendous views over some fields to the sea, and on clear days the unmistakable outline of Lundy could be seen – a greyish shape on the horizon, as unreachable as a distant star. The sight of it made Jenny ache with home-sickness, but the thought that Lundy was watching over her made her try even harder to play well.

Saturday afternoons at St Anne's were devoted to matches. Girls picked for teams played visiting teams from other schools, or escaped on coach journeys to play an away-match.

On Thursday afternoons the lists were put up, showing the teams for the following Saturday.

If you were picked for a team, you'd made it. Popularity was assured, as long as you didn't let the team down. Team members had a special Match Tea afterwards, which was always good because the competition between schools to produce the best tea was almost as fierce as the competition to win matches.

If you weren't picked for a team you were a nobody, and

even the teachers didn't seem to care what you did on Saturday afternoon. You certainly didn't get any Match Tea.

On the third Thursday of term, Jenny became popular.

"Well done, Jenny! You're Right Defence! Welcome to the team!" said Lucinda, the goddess-like Team Captain, emerging from the scrum around the notice board.

Other girls crowded round Jenny, offering congratulations and instant friendship.

Jenny had made it!

At supper that night she sat with her new friends. They seemed impressed by her knowledge of horses and riding. She didn't tell them it came almost entirely from books.

Jenny avoided looking at the corner table where her old friends sat, and at the empty place they'd been saving for her.

The match on Saturday was an away-match at a school near Barnstaple.

Jenny climbed onto the coach, and slid into a double seat halfway down while the other girls noisily bagged seats and shouted for their best friends to join them. Not for the first time, Jenny felt alone and insecure amongst the fickle, exciting gang she now called her friends. She missed thoughtful, dependable Fran more than she cared to admit.

The seats, covered with a material like thin carpet, felt rough against her bare legs and smelt of stale cigarette smoke. The smell reminded Jenny of the Tavern after a good party. She smiled. In her Sunday letter home she'd have to tell Dad she now liked stale cigarette smoke, because it reminded her of Lundy. He'd think that was hilarious. She was always nagging him to stop smoking.

"What's the joke, then?"

Jenny jumped, woken from her daydream. "What?"

Lucinda stood in the narrow aisle by Jenny's seat, resplendent in her Team Captain's uniform. "Something must be funny. You're grinning like a Cheshire cat." Before Jenny could attempt an explanation, she said, "Budge up. I usually sit with Wizzy, but she's not around at the moment, so I'd better sit with you."

Flustered, and deeply honoured, Jenny beamed at Lucinda and obligingly budged up, squashing herself against the cold window and leaving at least three-quarters of the seat free.

"Um, who's Wizzy?" Jenny asked, trying to find something to talk about.

Lucinda laughed. "You must be the only girl in North Devon who doesn't know Wizzy! She's in all the Pony Club teams *and* the county lacrosse team. We always win lax matches when she's in the team. Everyone loves Wizzy. We're all lost without her."

The coach started with a shudder, and rumbled down the school drive.

"Has she gone to a different school, then?"

"Of course not! Haven't you heard? It was simply *awful!*" Lucinda exclaimed, gripping Jenny's arm. "Her father bought her this new pony. Apparently someone said it was a fantastic jumper, so he bought it unseen. I suppose he wanted to snap it up before anyone else got the chance. Anyway, it turned out to be a *complete* nut-case! It attacked Wizzy and nearly killed her, the brute. She ended up in hospital with a broken arm, a broken collar bone, broken ribs - you name it, she broke it! She's on the mend now, thank goodness, but it looks as if she won't come back to school until after half term. Poor old Wizzy! It was *such* a disappointment, quite apart from anything else. It's *so* difficult to find a pony to take you up to the next level when you're competitive, isn't it?"

Jenny nodded wisely, hoping that was the correct response. You haven't seen Midnight jumping, she thought. Her heart missed a beat, as it did whenever she dared think about him.

"Oh well, she'll just have to make do with Creo until she finds something better," said Lucinda. Then she knelt on her seat, and joined in an animated conversation with the girls in the seats behind.

The bus turned out of the school drive, and they entered the outside world.

Lucinda ignored Jenny for the rest of the trip, apart from pointing at a large house on top of a hill and saying, "Look! There's Wizzy's house!"

Jenny spent most of the time gazing out of the window, trying to remember where she'd heard of a pony called Creo. The name rang a bell, but she couldn't think why.

CHAPTER FIFTEEN

Dear Dad,

I hope you are well. I am very well. I played Right Defence in a match against The Grange yesterday, and we won 10-4. It was fun, and the tea was delishious. I've made lots of new friends, and Miss Munro says I'm an asset to the lax team.

We can't do riding at the moment because the horses are ill, so I haven't had a chance to wear the polo neck, hat and jods you gave me.

How's Meg? Give her a pat from me.

Guess what? I've decided I like the smell of cigarette smoke, because it reminds me of the Tavern and you!

Say hello to everyone from me. Make sure you look after Gale.

Please write.
Love from
Jenny

Jenny folded her obligatory Sunday letter home, put it into an envelope and addressed it, being careful not to stick the flap down because letters home had to be inspected by Miss Nash. Then she wrote to Mrs Hamilton, giving a goal-by-goal account of the victorious lax match.

Most of the girls wrote at least six letters every Sunday, and received a steady stream of replies throughout the week. Jenny had received two letters in three weeks: one from her father and one from Mrs Hamilton. More than anything she longed for a letter from Ben, but she was too shy to make the first move and write to him. Besides, she didn't know his address.

Miss Nash was Jenny's Housemistress. She was also the teacher in charge of the post, and she relished this powerful position, well-aware that the arrival of the post was the highlight of the girls' day. Every morning she made them wait while she carefully placed the final few letters in their alphabetical pigeon-holes in the Great Hall, even though she'd had plenty of time to sort the letters by morning break. Then she stood back and watched, eagle-eyed, as the girls swooped in on the pigeon-holes like a flock of gulls squabbling behind a trawler.

On Tuesday there was a letter for Jenny. It was her letter home, with SEE ME written in red ink on the envelope. The envelope was empty. Jenny stood staring at it, bewildered.

"Ooh! Who's been a naughty girl?" Lucinda giggled, looking over Jenny's shoulder.

"Are you all right, Jenny?" Fran asked. "You look as white as a sheet!"

"Look," Jenny said, showing her the envelope. Her hands shook. "Do you think something awful has happened at home?"

"Don't worry. I expect it's just old Nashers being super-petty. She returned my letter home last week because it had a split infinitive. Can you beat it?"

"I expect I probably can," Jenny said, smiling.

I'm so sorry I abandoned you, Fran. You're a better

friend than any of the others. She wanted to say it, but she just thought it.

"Look," Fran said, "she's going into her study now. Good luck! Take your gas mask!"

Jenny held her nose and made a comic face. "Thanks!" She went over to the heavy oak door, and knocked hesitantly.

"Come in!"

She entered Miss Nash's lair, with its rigorously polished wood and neatly ordered bookshelves, clutching her empty envelope.

"Ah, Jennifer. Jennifer Medway," Miss Nash said.

"Um, you wanted to see me." Jenny felt like a fish caught on a hook.

"You wanted to see me, *Miss Nash*, without the 'um', if you please," Miss Nash corrected, obviously enjoying herself. She intended to reel in Jenny slowly.

"You wanted to see me, Miss Nash."

"I did indeed. Come and sit down."

As she neared the desk, Jenny couldn't help wrinkling her nose. Miss Nash was famous for her bad breath. Jenny handed her the envelope.

"Ah, yes. Your letter." With deliberation, Miss Nash pulled out the centre drawer of her large desk and retrieved Jenny's letter home. "Your letter," she repeated.

"If you think I've been smoking because I told Dad I like the smell of cigarettes, I haven't. The seats on the coach smelt of stale smoke, and it reminded me of the Tavern," Jenny said quickly.

Miss Nash was momentarily thrown off course, but she quickly regained her composure. She looked over the top of her glasses, which seemed permanently lodged between two convenient lumps on her bony nose. "I hope you're not telling me you frequent this den of iniquity on Lundy Island – this, Tavern?"

Jenny longed to correct Miss Nash, but she didn't dare. Mr Bonham always insisted that to call Lundy 'Lundy Island' was wrong, because the name was derived from *lundi*, meaning puffin, and *ey*, meaning island.

She said, "Of course I go to the Tavern. It's the place where everyone on Lundy meets up. We have tremendous parties. I mean, I mean, it's like – like a village hall."

"I see," said Miss Nash doubtfully. She handed Jenny's letter back to her and said, "Kindly re-write your letter to your father, making it crystal-clear that you have not taken up smoking."

Jenny wanted to giggle.

"And attend to the other corrections, as I have indicated. Do not use slang in your letters – it is vulgar – and if you do not know how to spell, use your dictionary."

Jenny glanced down at her letter. The words *lax* and *jods* had been circled in red ink, and so had *delishious*. "Yes, Miss Nash. Can I go now?"

"I'm sure you *can* go, but you *may* not," corrected Miss Nash.

"Sorry, Miss Nash. *May* I go now?" Jenny asked with exaggerated politeness.

"No, you may not. This letter arrived today, and I assume you answer to the name of Jenny, brackets, New Girl, close brackets," Miss Nash said, holding out a large envelope in her mottled, claw-like hands.

Jenny took the envelope, her heart racing. She didn't recognise the rather childish writing on the envelope, *Jenny* (*New Girl*), *St Anne's School*, *North Devon*, but she felt sure it was from Ben. He'd said he wasn't very good at reading and writing. He obviously wasn't good at addressing, either. Her spirits soared. "Thank you, Miss Nash! May I go now?"

A bell rang out, signalling the end of morning break.

"You may," Miss Nash replied.

The rest of the morning was torture, without a single opportunity to look inside the mysterious letter. She couldn't concentrate, and was told off several times for not paying attention. What had Ben sent her? Perhaps he'd found Midnight. Perhaps – perhaps – oh, come on, lunchtime!

After morning lessons, she hid in the changing rooms until everyone had gone to lunch.

Hunger was a price worth paying for being so blissfully alone. She opened her locker, and took out the envelope. Her fingers trembled as she eased it open. Barely able to contain her excitement, she peered inside.

Her stamps! She couldn't believe it. The Lundy stamps Mr Bonham had given her – the complete sheet of them, none the worse for wear.

The torn-out page of an exercise book fluttered to the ground as she pulled the stamps out of their envelope. She picked it up, and read:

Dear Jenny,

I hope you are well. I didn't go back on my word. Camilla and Will followed you that day when Midnight trapped me. They told Mummy and Daddy about it.

Here are your stamps.

The boys at my school all have girlfriends who write to them. Will you be my girlfriend?

We don't have to hold hands or anything. You can write to me and I can write to you.

Love from
Hector Bonham

PS My address is Hornborough School, Little Fanstead, Oxfordshire. I hope I got yours right.

Jenny sat on the slatted wooden bench by her peg, surrounded by mucky art overalls and sweaty games kits, and read, then re-read the letter in disbelief. Part of her hated Hector for not being Ben, and part of her hated him for being Hector, but she found his peculiar sense of honour rather touching. And letters from Hector would be better than no letters at all. She decided she would write to him, but she definitely wouldn't go as far as calling herself his girlfriend. She put his letter back in the envelope, together with the stamps, and hid them safely in her locker.

CHAPTER SIXTEEN

First Jenny counted the weeks, then the days, then the hours until half term. She thought she'd burst with the effort of waiting. It was all planned; she'd take a taxi and catch the boat from Bideford Quay to Lundy on the Friday afternoon. Then she'd return on the boat the following Thursday with Mrs Hamilton. They would stay in the hotel in Bideford until Sunday, when everyone returned to school. Somehow Jenny would have to rescue Midnight in those two whole precious days. It would be her only chance before the Barnstaple horse sales. The 'how' bit of somehow was still at the planning stage, unfortunately. A major stumbling block would be Mrs Hamilton.

On Thursday the wind, which had been a light south-westerly all week, backed to a south-easterly direction, and increased to force six.

Jenny lay in bed, praying the wind would go away.

It didn't.

Matron came into the dorm after First Bell. "Jennifer, Miss Nash would like to see you in her study as soon as possible," she said, looking deeply apologetic.

Jenny knew what it was about. She went with a heavy heart.

Miss Nash was almost kind. "I am sorry Jennifer, but your boat has been cancelled due to the bad weather.

I gather that an easterly wind is particularly perilous when attempting to land on Lundy Island. I am afraid you will have to stay here with me, as you have no relations nearby. I know it must be a disappointment for you, as it is for me, but we will make the best of it, shall we not?"

A great lump lodged in Jenny's throat. She managed to force out a hoarse, "Thank you, Miss Nash," and then bolted for the door as hot tears started to fall.

Jenny's friends appeared sympathetic about her plight, but there was a touch of glee in their voices as they talked about it over breakfast, in-between chatting excitedly about their plans for half term. Jenny wanted to scream.

She felt a tap on her shoulder, and looked round.

It was Fran. "I heard about the boat, Jenny. You can always come and stay with me, if you like," she said.

The girls round the table stopped talking and looked at Jenny, waiting eagerly for her response.

She knew what they thought of Fran: swotty, hopeless at games - a nobody. Jenny had become a somebody. "Thanks, but I'd rather stay here," she said.

The cars arrived in droves after lunch. Jenny watched out of her dormitory window, burning with jealousy as girls hugged their parents, and were whisked away to freedom. She saw Fran's parents arrive in the black Bentley, and remembered how kind they'd been. She could have been with them now if she hadn't been so vile. She hated the person she'd become.

The last car drove away. Silence.

Jenny flopped onto her bed, and closed her eyes. The ordeal of half term with Miss Nash had begun.

She sighed, got up and looked out of the window again. She felt like a princess imprisoned in a wicked witch's castle, except she was a pretty horrible princess. No prince in his right mind would want to save her.

A dark grey car came up the drive, and stopped outside the main entrance to the school. It was much smaller and older than the parents' cars which Jenny had seen all day. Perhaps it belonged to the Head Gardener, or the Bursar. Jenny watched as a neatly dressed, tall, slim gentleman with grey hair got out and shut the car door with careful precision. He looked strangely familiar.

It couldn't be. It *was!* "Albert!" Jenny shouted, leaping down the stairs to the Great Hall two-at-a-time. Her prince *had* come! Albert had come to rescue her!

"Mr Hamilton told the Coastguards at Hartland that you were stranded at school for half term, and they contacted me straight away to see what could be done," Albert explained as they drove out of the school gates. "As it happens, I'm home this week, so it's all tied in very nicely."

Jenny looked at the PK, and smiled. He was a little bit of Lundy, right there beside her – the next best thing to going home.

He drove with careful precision. His car, though obviously quite old, was as clean and polished as a lighthouse.

"It's funny to think you've got a car," she said. "In fact, it's funny to think you live here at all. I hadn't imagined you anywhere but Lundy."

Albert laughed. "And look at you in your school uniform! What happened to the tomboy I used to know?"

"Oh, she's still here, itching to get out."

The Scoines family's home was a pretty whitewashed cottage with blue window frames and window boxes, just by the sea in Appledore. Unlike the bare South Light, it was full of trinkets, family photos, intricate model ships made by Albert and elaborate soft furnishings made by Mrs Scoines. Like the South Light, the whole place was clean and tidy, with a proper place for everything.

Mrs Scoines welcomed Jenny with a radiant smile and a motherly hug. She was as short and round as Albert was tall and thin. Jenny could see why Ben had turned out stockier than his father.

"I've given you Eileen's old room, in the attic," Mrs Scoines said. "I hope you like it."

Jenny felt sure she'd like any room in the cosy cottage. Ben had talked about Eileen when they were on Lundy. She was Ben's older sister, who'd married and moved to Canada.

"Would you like a cup of tea, before I show you to your room?" Mrs Scoines asked. She had already poured one out. "Milk and sugar? Albert always has it with condensed milk. He says real milk doesn't taste right. He's spent too long in a lighthouse!"

"Ooh, condensed milk would be lovely, thank you."

The sweet, mellow tea tasted wonderful – totally different from the harsh, dark liquid which passed for tea at school. It took Jenny back to that sunny morning at the North Light, the first day she met Ben.

As if reading her mind, Ben walked through the door. His face creased into the most wonderful smile. "Jenny!" He walked straight over and hugged her, then stepped back to look at her. "Blimey! You *do* look posh! Guess what? I've got the weekend off, so I'll be able to show you the *real* North Devon. Once we've got you into some proper clothes, that is – we don't want to scare the natives, do we?"

All Jenny's fears that things would be different between them on the mainland vanished.

After tea, Jenny and Ben walked along the cobbled streets of Appledore and stood watching the tide as it raced out, blown by the wind.

At last Jenny could tell Ben about Midnight, and school, and the girls who kept their ponies at the riding stables, and Hector's letter with the stamps in it – leaving out the part where he'd asked her to be his girlfriend. Her words spilled out in an unstoppable torrent, like the water rushing out to sea in front of them. "So you see," she said finally, "I've got it all worked out. Tomorrow I'll sell the stamps, and hopefully that will give me enough money to buy Midnight from Dobbin and keep him at livery at Home Farm."

"Simple!" Ben teased. "Or as posh girls say, *easy-peasy!*"

Jenny punched him. "Don't mock! This is serious!"

Ben raised his arms and pretended to look frightened. "Okay! Okay! I surrender! I'll do anything you say!"

"Good! You'll help me, then?"

"Well, if you're sure about all this," said Ben. "I think the first thing we should do is pay Uncle Bob, a visit. He's really my Godfather, but I've always called him Uncle Bob. He lives in Bideford, and he's an expert on stamps and all things collectible to do with Lundy. I know we can trust him to give you a good price. We'll bike there first thing tomorrow. You can borrow Mum's bike, I'm sure."

"Um, I've never ridden a bike before," Jenny said doubtfully. "They're not much use on Lundy, you see."

Ben smiled. "Okay, first I'll teach you to ride a bike, *then* we'll pay Uncle Bob a visit."

Jenny giggled. "Bob's your uncle," she said.

"Yes, he is. Why's it so funny?"

"It's something Mrs Hamilton says a lot. I think it means no problem, or *easy-peasy.*"

They both laughed, and Jenny suddenly felt sure everything would turn out all right. She'd learn how to ride a bike, sell the stamps for lots of money, and then buy Midnight, Bob's your uncle.

Following a brief lesson in riding a bike – a crash course in more ways than one – Jenny cycled behind Ben, wobbling only occasionally, all the way to Bideford. The thought she could be Midnight's owner by nightfall spurred her on.

Bob Jenkins was a large, jovial man who looked and dressed more like a fisherman than a stamp collector. He had a small antiques and stamp shop, aptly called Aladdin's Cave, up a backstreet in Bideford.

"This is like finding buried treasure!" he said to Jenny when she showed him the stamps. "Where on earth did you get them?"

"Um, Mr Bonham gave them to me, thinking I collect stamps, but I don't anymore," Jenny said, hoping it didn't sound ungrateful.

Bob chuckled. "Well, you can't get a better provenance than that! But why not keep them anyway, as an investment? They're bound to increase in value."

"I need to buy a pony. A Lundy pony."

He chuckled again. "You girls, you're all the same! If you're not careful, you'll turn out like Rose, my little sister. You ought to meet her sometime, if you like Lundy ponies. She's obsessed! I think it started when she bought one for her children ages ago – a lovely little mare called Kestrel, I seem to remember. The children did all sorts of things with her, and she was forever winning prizes. Anyway, Rose kept that one, and bought another, and another, and now she's gathered together quite a herd of them. She collects ponies like I collect antiques. Come to think of it, most of her ponies *are* antiques! She specialises in buying the old crocks from Barnstaple Market every year, because she feels sorry for them and doesn't want them to go for meat. It's lucky she's got an understanding husband who owns a large chunk of Bodmin Moor, that's all I can say! No, young Jenny, I'd keep your stamps, if I were you. They'll be far less trouble than a pony."

Jenny thanked him for the advice, but said she was quite sure she wanted to buy the pony, and selling the stamps was her only option.

To her delight, he gave her more money than she'd dared hope for. Real money, in five and ten-pound notes, from an impressive safe in his cluttered back room.

Ben and Jenny accepted an offer of tea and cake, and then they set off back to Appledore and Dobbin's yard.

Jenny's wobbles on the bike were now more to do with excitement than inexperience.

Dobbin's yard wasn't at all as Jenny had imagined. She'd expected dirty stables and abused horses, but Ben parked his bike outside some bright white gates leading to an impressive courtyard, surrounded on three sides by airy looseboxes with newly painted dark green doors and window frames. The whole place looked more like a racing stables than a dealer's yard.

"You're sure we've come to the right place?" Jenny asked, surveying the inquisitive horses which popped their heads over their stable doors, ears pricked and eyes bright. They looked well and happy. None of them looked like Midnight.

"Quite sure." Ben gave Jenny a reassuring pat on the back. "Only the best for Midnight."

Jenny didn't feel at all reassured. She felt out of her depth.

An Alsatian dog appeared, barking.

"Duke! Go and lie down!" Dobbin shouted, emerging from a room in the centre of the stable block, which Jenny guessed was the tack room. He saw the visitors, raised a hand in greeting and hurried over. His welcoming smile changed to a frown as he recognised Jenny. "What are you doing here?" he snapped.

"Where's Midnight? I can't see him," Jenny blurted out. It wasn't what she'd meant to say, not straight away like that, but she couldn't help it.

"Lord knows."

I can't have heard him correctly, Jenny thought. "Um, sorry?"

"I said Lord knows," Dobbin repeated slowly, as if talking to an idiot. "I don't know, and I most definitely don't care."

Immobilised with shock, Jenny stared at him. "But, but, where, um, where..."

Ben stepped in. "Where's he gone, then? Did you sell him to someone?"

"Too right, I did. To a man with more money than sense. He sent his groom down with a horsebox soon after we arrived back here. Wanted him just like that - unseen, no questions asked. Heard he was the most brilliant jumping pony, apparently. Wish all my customers were so foolish."

"But, but you must have *told* him Midnight wasn't broken to ride or anything!" Jenny exclaimed. A little voice in the back of her mind reminded her she hadn't told Isabella, but she informed the little voice this was different. *This* was dishonest.

"If they don't ask, don't tell. First rule of horse trading. Now, with that pearl of wisdom to send you on your way, I'll wish you a safe journey back to Lundy."

"Have you got the address of the person who bought Midnight?" Ben asked.

"Even if I had, I wouldn't give it to you, boy. Customer confidentiality. I doubt Midnight's there, anyway. Didn't live up to expectations, by all accounts. Put the man's daughter in hospital. Bad news, that pony. He's probably gone to Fremington by now. Best place for him." He turned and walked away.

"Whereabouts in Fremington?" Jenny called after him.

Still walking, he turned his head slightly and said, "Where do you think?"

"Come on, Jenny. Let's go," Ben said. "Let's go home."

"But why won't he tell us where Midnight is in Fremington?" Jenny protested.

Ben put his arm round her shoulder, as if trying to protect her from the shock of what he was about to tell her. "Because he meant the abattoir in Fremington," he said.

That night Jenny couldn't sleep. She lay in bed in her cosy attic room, and stared at the sloping ceiling. Terrible thoughts tormented her, daring her to face the truth.

The truth, she now realised, was that Wizzy was Isabella Wagstaff. Jenny had told Wizzy she rode Midnight. Jenny had told Wizzy he was a fantastic jumper. Although both those things were true separately, together they made a lie so wicked that it had probably resulted in Midnight's death. Wizzy could have been killed, too, by all accounts.

Jenny turned first one way, then the other. The patchwork quilt slid off the bed and slumped onto the floor.

She shivered, and closed her eyes tight. Why was she so vain and *hateful?* Why was she such a liar? Her lies weren't white lies, they were cowardly and black, with terrible consequences. She'd lied to Wizzy to impress her. She'd lied to Fran to remain popular, whatever that meant. Worst of all, she'd lied to Midnight, but he'd been clever enough to see right through her; she'd seen it in his eye when she'd abandoned him on the Landing Beach.

I am responsible. The words haunted her all night.

CHAPTER SEVENTEEN

"Are you all right, Jenny? You look a bit under-the-weather," Mrs Scoines said at the breakfast table the following morning.

"Oh, I'm fine, thanks. I just had a bad dream last night. It kept me awake," Jenny replied.

Ben raised his eyebrows.

He doesn't know the half of it, she thought. He'll hate me, but I'll have to tell him.

"We can just stay here today, if you want. It's Sunday, so there's not much going on anywhere," said Ben.

"No. Let's go for a bike ride," Jenny said. "As long as you don't mind me borrowing your bike, Mrs Scoines."

She looked pleased. "Not a bit! You seem to have taken to cycling like a duck to water. I'll make you some sandwiches. By the way, do call me Ada. It seems silly for you to call me Mrs Scoines when you call Albert by his Christian name."

"Thank you, um, Ada," Jenny said shyly. On Lundy it seemed natural for her to call everyone by their Christian names – apart from Mr and Mrs Hamilton and Mr and Mrs Bonham, of course. And she didn't call Major Bathurst 'Batty' to his face, although most of the adults did. However, after the stuffy formality of school it seemed rude to call any adults by their Christian names, even Albert.

"Okay, where to?" Ben asked as they set off, bumping down the cobbled street which led to the main road out of Appledore.

"St Anne's," Jenny said.

"Why there, of all places?"

"I'll tell you on the way. I'm afraid I've got quite a lot of explaining to do."

It was surprisingly easy to talk as they rode along side-by-side. Jenny wanted Ben to know everything, even if it made him like her less. She talked all the way to the gates of St Anne's School.

"Blimey!" Ben said. "What bad luck."

Jenny was taken aback. "What do you mean?"

"Well, we all make mistakes, but usually we get away with them. All yours have come back to bite you on the bum."

They looked at each other, started laughing and then couldn't stop. Tears of laughter and relief flowed from Jenny's eyes.

"You will make it up to Fran, though, won't you?" Ben said at last. "It sounds as if she's had a pretty raw deal."

Jenny scuffed the tarmac with her foot. "I know. I'll try, but I doubt whether she'll want anything to do with me, after the way I treated her."

Ben sighed. "I'm so glad I've finished with all that school nonsense," he said. "Okay, then. Where to now? You don't seriously want to go in there, do you?" He pointed at the school drive.

"No fear! I wanted to start from here because there's a chance, just a chance, we may be able to find Midnight, if he's still alive. You see, Lucinda pointed out Wizzy's house to me on our way to a lax match against The Grange. If we can retrace the route, I'm sure I'll recognise the house."

"It's worth a try," said Ben. "Where's The Grange?"

"That's the problem. I don't know exactly, but I'll try to

remember as we go along. I spent most of the journey looking out of the window, because Lucinda was gossiping with the girls behind."

"Let's have a sandwich; this could be a long day," said Ben.

One of Robert Medway's sayings was, "If you think something's going to be difficult it'll take a few minutes, and if you think something's going to be easy it'll take all day."

Finding Wizzy's house took about twenty minutes, no problem.

"Bob's your uncle!" Jenny exclaimed as they approached some closed wrought iron gates set in a curved stone wall. "This is it." She got off her bike, and read the name carved into a large stone slab, "Rockleigh Manor."

A drive flanked by post-and-rail fencing led to an impressive stone-built house which, by the looks of it, was still under construction. It had been memorable to Jenny because it looked like a grander version of Millcombe, the Bonham's house on Lundy.

"What now?" asked Ben.

"We go in," said Jenny, trying to sound confident.

"Ladies first," Ben said, bowing with mock gallantry.

What little confidence Jenny had evaporated as they walked up the drive, pushing their bikes.

"Can I help you, love?" asked a builder, climbing down from his ladder.

"Um, we're looking for the stables, please," Jenny said.

"There ain't no public stables here, y'know. Just private ones, like."

"Yes, we know. We've come to see Mr, um, Wagstaff."

The builder turned to Ben. "Oh, right! You're the new groom! The stables are round the back there, see? The boss is expecting you. Good luck, mate. You'll need it." Then he climbed back up the ladder again.

Jenny and Ben looked at each other, and grinned sheepishly.

As they walked round to the stables, Ben said quietly, "If they don't ask, don't tell. First rule of horse trading."

The stable yard was newly built, but already looked shabby. The concrete was strewn with muck and straw, a dung fork and broom lay abandoned in the middle of the yard and a couple of empty buckets rolled around in a sudden gust of wind. Jenny instinctively looked up. Large thunder clouds loomed overhead.

"I'll have this place looking better in no time!" said Ben.

"Ben! You're not actually looking for a job, remember? We're looking for Midnight!" Jenny hissed, exasperated.

"Oh dear, I forgot!" Ben teased. His smile vanished. "Er, hello, sir."

Jenny turned round. Mr Wagstaff strode towards them. "There you are! You'd better not make a habit of being late!" he barked. "Come into my office immediately."

"But..."

"For goodness sake, boy! Hurry! I haven't got all day!" Mr Wagstaff indicated to Jenny. "You'd better bring your sister in with you. It's starting to rain."

At that moment there was a crack of thunder and an almost simultaneous flash of lightning, and huge raindrops plummeted down. They ran to the house, with no time to explain the purpose of their visit.

Mr Wagstaff's office was obviously designed to cope with a great deal of paperwork. There were shelves full of files, rows of filing cabinets and tables with bulging in-trays. Everything was functional. Where Mr Hamilton would have had a good painting on his office wall, Mr Wagstaff had diagrams and, oddly, photos of large wastelands with heavy machinery in them. There seemed to be paper everywhere, but there were also rocks. Lumps of rock acted as paperweights on several tables, including a long central table which had a large map rolled out on it.

Jenny instantly realised the map was of Lundy. She edged nearer to get a closer look. The East Sideland from Quarter Wall Bay to Tibbett's Point had red lines and symbols all over it, and it looked as if Quarry Bay had been transformed into a small harbour protected by sea walls, complete with a quay and jetty. She was looking at a plan to open up and expand the old quarries! How dare Mr Wagstaff *consider* such a thing? Lundy didn't even belong to him!

Mr Wagstaff ended his brief interview with Ben. "Right, I've just got time to show you the stables. We'll have to be quick, though. I'm a very busy man," he said, striding past Jenny and out of the door.

They followed him obediently.

The thunderstorm had passed, leaving glistening grass and a damp earth smell in its wake.

They entered the yard, and stopped outside a stable with 'Creo' on a nameplate above the door.

"My daughter's pony. Been a good servant. Too small for her now," Mr Wagstaff said, and moved on to the next stable.

Jenny peered inside, and saw a classy-looking bright chestnut pony with a white blaze standing in the corner. It had no intention of coming up to say hello.

They walked hastily down the line of stables, pausing by each one for a brief description of the occupant. The horses looked bored, bad-tempered or both. The last stable appeared to be unused; both doors were shut.

No Midnight. Jenny felt numb.

"Well, that's that. Any questions?" Mr Wagstaff asked.

"Er, yes. Do you have a pony called Midnight here, sir?" Ben asked.

"Why?" Mr Wagstaff seemed suspicious.

"Oh, I heard he's a good jumper."

He gave a dry laugh. "That's just what I heard, too. He's also a killer. Tried to kill my daughter. Didn't succeed, thank God. We've persevered with him, as anyone would with such an expensive animal, but he just gets worse and worse. He's not right in the head. I'm afraid he's a dead loss – or he will be when the knackerman finally turns up." He glanced at his watch. "Everyone seems to be late today. It's ridiculous how the whole world grinds to a halt on a Sunday. It should be a working day like any other."

"I'll buy him," Jenny said, "for double what the knackerman would have given you."

"*What?*" Mr Wagstaff had obviously forgotten Jenny was there. Now he stared at her, astonished.

She stared back, like a rabbit overshadowed by a bird of prey, paralysed with fear. For some reason, she noticed his tie and remembered Mrs Hamilton saying, 'You can tell a gentleman by the way he knots his tie'.

Tut, tut, Mr Wagstaff, she thought. You obviously haven't mastered the Windsor knot. "I said I'll buy him," she said, with new-found courage.

"And *who* are *you?*"

Jenny fixed her eyes on his sloppy tie. "I'm Jenny Medway. I live on Lundy. I met Isabella last summer when you came to Lundy on – um – business, and I'm afraid I may have let her think Midnight was broken to ride when he wasn't really. I used to sit on his back as he wandered around, but that isn't exactly riding, is it? But he really can jump! He used to jump all over the place on Lundy, I swear."

Mr Wagstaff looked astounded. There was a long silence.

Water dripped from the gutters.

"No, it's out of the question," he said finally. "Quite apart from anything else, you'd never be able to afford him. Even at knacker price he's worth fifteen pounds."

Jenny knew that was a bit steep, but she didn't argue. She pulled the money from her anorak pocket and counted it out. "There. That should do it," she said, handing thirty pounds to Mr Wagstaff. She offered her hand. "Deal?"

They shook on the deal just as the knackerman's lorry rumbled up the drive.

Soon he rumbled away again, with five pounds in his pocket for his wasted journey.

"That was a bit generous!" Ben hissed in her ear. "You'll have no money left at this rate!"

Jenny planned to keep Midnight at Home Farm, but she hadn't asked them yet. Perhaps he could stay put for a few days while she got it all sorted out.

"I'm terribly late for a meeting," Mr Wagstaff said. "The pony's in there." He pointed to the end stable. "I want him gone by this evening. If you open the top door he'll jump out, and if you go in with him he'll attack you. Don't say I didn't warn you." He looked at Ben. "You didn't want that job, did you?"

"I'm afraid not, sir."

"Pity. Goodbye, then. And good luck with Midnight. You're welcome to him."

Jenny almost began to like the man, until she saw Midnight.

With a thumping heart, Jenny drew back the bolts on the top half of the stable door. As she opened the door, a stench of stale urine hit her. "Midnight," she called softly. "Hello, old boy. It's me, Jenny. Remem..."

Her words were cut short as Midnight's head snaked out, and his body crashed against the shut door below.

She leapt back, knocking into Ben. Midnight's yellow teeth snapped shut so close to her head that she could feel the air tremble.

He lunged again, teeth bared, eyes rolling.

Whatever Jenny had expected, it hadn't been this. What on earth had happened to him? He'd gone mad! There wasn't even a flicker of recognition in those sunken, demonic eyes.

"He doesn't know me!" Jenny cried. "Or – or perhaps he does! Perhaps he knows *exactly* who I am! I'm the one who betrayed him! No wonder he hates me so much!" She clung to Ben, wailing like a wounded animal.

At last she managed to pull herself together. "What are we going to do?" she said.

"Do you think you'll be all right if we split up and go in different directions?" Ben asked. "I'll bike back to Bideford, and get a livestock lorry to come and pick up Midnight. You'd better go to that riding place of yours, to see whether they'll have him."

Home Farm Equestrian Centre was a hive of activity. One ride had just come back, and another was preparing to go out. Children and ponies of all shapes and sizes filled the yard.

Jenny instantly loved the place. It looked like a storybook riding school. Please let it be all right, she thought, as she walked hesitantly into the yard. Please let them say yes! She felt lost without Ben. In fact, she wouldn't have gone in at all if she hadn't been so desperate to find somewhere for Midnight.

"May I help you?" A slim, efficient-looking lady wearing riding clothes approached with a welcoming smile.

"Um, I've heard you have ponies to stay here on, er, livery," Jenny said.

"Yes, we do sometimes. It depends on the pony. What sort of livery do you require?"

Jenny felt foolish. "Um, what are the sorts?"

"Well, there's working livery, part livery or full livery," the lady explained patiently.

"Which is the cheapest?"

"Working livery. We pay for your pony's keep, and you pay for the farrier and any vets bills."

"That sounds ideal," Jenny said.

"And in return," the lady continued, "we use your pony for riding lessons."

"Um, not so ideal. You see, my pony isn't broken to ride or anything. In fact, he doesn't really like people at all at the moment."

The lady looked thoughtful. "I see," she said slowly. "So you'd like him to come here to be broken in? I'm afraid that's even more expensive than full livery. How old is your pony?"

Jenny tried to work it out. "I think about twenty-four," she said.

"Ah," said the lady. "That's a bit old for..."

"Oh, and I forgot to say, he's a stallion," Jenny said, with a feeling of impending doom. Tears ran down her face. She rubbed her eyes furiously, but they just wouldn't stop. "P-Poor M-Midnight! He h-hates me! It's all my f-fault!" she stammered between sobs.

The ponies were standing in line, ready to go for a ride.

"Jackie!" the lady called. "Take Emma with you to shut the gates. You'd better go on without me." Then she turned back to Jenny. "I think we need a mug of tea and a chat, don't you?"

"Y-yes p-please," Jenny said.

It turned out that the efficient-looking lady, who was called

Mrs Moat, owned Home Farm with her husband. She was a riding teacher, and he was a farmer.

Mrs Moat came up with an excellent idea: Midnight could be kept out in a field away from the riding stables, with a bunch of young steers for company, until Jenny could find him a good home somewhere. Jenny would have to pay for his share of the hay, which would be taken to the field once a day, but that was all.

Although she hardly knew the lady, Jenny hugged her.

Mrs Moat insisted on driving Jenny back to Rockleigh Manor. "We'll take the horse lorry, just in case your friend hasn't managed to find any transport," Mrs Moat said. "Pop your bike in the back, if you like."

Ben was waiting for Jenny by the stable yard at Rockleigh Manor. His face lit up when he saw the horse lorry. "Thank goodness for that! I got half way to Bideford, and remembered it was Sunday and all the transport businesses would be shut. I didn't know what to do!"

To Jenny's relief, Mrs Moat took control. She backed the lorry expertly into the stable yard, shut the yard gate and lowered the lorry ramp onto the ground just in front of Midnight's stable. She shut the top doors of the other stables, and told Jenny and Ben to stand on the other side of the gate. Then, armed with a pitchfork, 'just in case', she opened both the doors to Midnight's stable.

Nothing happened.

"It'll take him a bit of time to pluck up the courage to come out," said Mrs Moat. She stepped back a few paces, leaving more room.

She doesn't know Midnight, Jenny thought. He never lacks courage.

Jenny soon found out it was she who no longer knew Midnight. An emaciated pony gradually emerged, each trembling step a huge effort. Dried dung stuck to his body, partially hiding his many scars and patches of raw skin. He caught sight of Mrs Moat and froze, shaking all over. Then he jumped onto the lorry ramp, missed his footing, went down on his knees, scrambled up again, tripped, nearly went down again and somehow scrambled the rest of the way in.

Swiftly, but calmly, Mrs Moat lifted the lorry ramp and bolted it shut. "There's one terrified pony," she said. "Whoever did that to him should be locked in a dark shed without bedding, food or water, to give them a taste of their own medicine. It's a miracle he's survived."

The field was down on the marshes below Home Farm. It was large and flat, with a patch of rushes at one end.

Mrs Moat drove the lorry into the field, closed the gate and lowered the ramp. A herd of brown-coloured cattle loped up, and stood around gawping. Midnight stopped at the top of the ramp, trembling in an agony of indecision.

"Let's just go for a walk down the lane a minute, and leave him to it," said Mrs Moat.

They walked down the lane. The evening sunshine bathed everything in golden light.

"He will be all right, won't he?" Jenny asked anxiously.

"To be honest I don't know, Jenny. Luckily for me, I have little experience of horses which have been so badly treated. All I can say is that we'll do our best for him."

When they got back to the field, Midnight was grazing next to the cattle.

"Well, that's the first hurdle over with, anyway," said Mrs Moat. "I'll pop you both back to Appledore. Your bikes are in the lorry already, and it'll soon be dark."

"Thank you so much, Mrs Moat. I don't know what we would have done without you," said Ben.

"Oh, I expect you'd have managed somehow," Mrs Moat replied.

I doubt it, Jenny thought. Perhaps our luck's changing, Midnight.

CHAPTER EIGHTEEN

Ben had to go back to work on Monday.

Jenny accepted Ada's offer of sandwiches and the loan of her bike, and went to see Midnight.

She leant on the gate, and watched as he relentlessly cropped the grass, making up for weeks of starvation. I own him, she thought. I *own* Midnight! It was a dream come true, wasn't it? But looking at the pitiful, dirty creature that had once been so magnificent and proud only filled her with immense sadness; there was no joy in owning him if he hated her.

She climbed over the gate. She had all day - all week. If she spent time with him, and got a little closer every day, perhaps he'd learn to trust her again.

Very slowly, she walked towards him.

He walked away, ears back, tail swishing.

She followed him.

Suddenly he charged: ears flat against his head, teeth bared, body low.

Jenny fled for the gate, jumped over, tripped and lay sprawled in the lane. She hurt all over, but that was nothing compared with the utter despair she felt inside.

It started to rain. Jenny trudged up the lane, pushing the bike. She came to a T-junction, and hesitated. What on earth was she going to do for the rest of the day? The rain poured down. She turned left, towards Home Farm.

Mrs Moat soon put her to work cleaning tack, grooming ponies and mucking out stables; but it didn't feel like work. A boy called Peter and two girls called Emma and Sophie were holiday helpers, too. It was fun.

"Thanks for all your hard work," Mrs Moat said at the end of the day. "If you want to come and help for the rest of the week, I'll pay you with some free riding. That's how it works with the others."

So for the rest of the week Jenny spent most of her time at Home Farm, helping and learning how to ride. She also made time to go and see Midnight, but she never went into his field.

On Saturday afternoon Ben's work finished early, so he met Jenny at Home Farm. They biked down to Midnight's field together, and stood looking over the gate.

"He's definitely looking better," Ben said.

"Do you think so? I suppose it's more difficult for me to notice, because I've seen him every day," Jenny replied.

"Sorry I've had to work all week, but it sounds as if you've had a good time at Home Farm," Ben said. "I bet you never thought you'd own Midnight and know how to ride by the end of half term!"

Jenny laughed. "Oh, I'm still a beginner at riding. I can't even canter yet! In fact, the more I learn, the more I realise how little I know. For a start, I had no idea how long it took to break in horses. It's incredible that Midnight used to let me sit on him."

"He trusted you. That was the key," Ben said.

"And he doesn't trust me anymore," Jenny said forlornly. "Oh, Ben! How can I get that back? How can I get him to trust me again?"

"You'll get there. Just give it time," said Ben. "Look, would you like to come to the cinema tonight? My treat, as this is your last night of freedom. That James Bond film everyone's been talking about has finally reached the Odeon."

So Jenny saw her first film. It swept her away into another world, and for a while she forgot to worry about Midnight or school.

Before she left for school on Sunday afternoon, Jenny gave Albert two letters to take back to Lundy: one telling her father all about Midnight, and one telling Mrs Hamilton about Mr Wagstaff's plans for the quarries.

Albert drove Jenny back to school, and Ben came too. Jenny noticed several girls looking at him as he carried her bag up to the dormitory.

"He's rather nice! Is he your brother?" Susie asked when Ben had left.

"No. He's just a friend," Jenny replied.

"What? Your *boyfriend?*" Susie asked.

"No, just a good friend. It is possible to have a good friend who happens to be a boy, you know."

"Ooh! Temper! I don't believe you. I think he's your boyfriend," Susie insisted.

"Think what you like," said Jenny. In the cinema last night, sitting in the dark close to Ben, the thought had crossed her mind that one day he just might be.

Jenny wasted no time in finding Fran and apologising to her. Fran hugged her, and said it didn't matter one bit, as long as they were friends again.

At supper that night Jenny sat at the corner table with Fran, Alison, Pandora, Dorothy, Jane and Belinda. She'd forgotten what good company they were. She could be herself again. No more pretending.

Wizzy sat in Jenny's old place at the 'popular table'.

From the glances in her direction, Jenny could see they were talking about her, and she could also see she was no longer popular. The odd thing was that she didn't care.

The second half of the autumn term passed quickly. With Wizzy back in the lax team, Jenny was relegated to reserve, and was soon dropped altogether because she put a great deal of effort into playing badly. This meant she managed to avoid Wizzy and Lucinda as much as possible. It also meant she was free to walk down and see Midnight on Saturday afternoons. Every week he looked a bit better. He still avoided her, though, and she didn't dare go into the field.

The other highlight of each week was riding lessons. Jenny discovered she loved riding. In fact, she loved everything about horses. Sometimes, if Wizzy and Lucinda had been vile yet again or if Jenny felt especially homesick, she'd take her riding clothes out of her cupboard and smell them. The smell of horses always cheered her up.

At last it was the end of term. The weather was crisp and calm, and Jenny was aboard the boat to Lundy, wondering whether she was dreaming.

It was too cold to stand out on deck, so she sat on the wooden bench in the cabin. Her body jittered with excitement, but she didn't feel at all sick this time.

"It doesn't seem five minutes since I was bringing you over to start school," Captain Dover said, puffing on his pipe.

"Really? It seems a lifetime ago to me," Jenny replied.

He pointed ahead, pipe-in-hand. "There she is! There's Lundy."

Jenny jumped up and peered through the smoke-stained window. A hazy blue-grey silhouette lay ahead. She rushed out on deck. The cold air sliced into her clothes, but she hardly noticed. Transfixed, she watched as the island gained colour and slowly came into focus, until eventually she could make out each cove and headland. Landmarks stood along the long skyline: Tibbett's, the Old Light, the Church, the Castle, the South Light.... Everything in place, dear and familiar, greeting her like old friends. Last of all, Millcombe came into view as they turned and dropped anchor in the Landing Bay.

The boat slapped and clumped in the light swell, waiting for Robert Medway to manoeuvre the landing boat alongside.

The distant star Jenny had gazed at for so long had become real. She was home!

It was a Christmas full of surprises, some better than others.

For a start, the cottage was immaculate, with freshly baked cakes and scones on the table.

On Christmas Eve, even though it was bitterly cold, Jenny's father asked her to walk to Jenny's Cove with him.

They stood looking out to sea. The glassy surface of the Atlantic Ocean reflected the feeble winter sun, and scarcely rippled where it met the jagged coastline. The dark cliffs, so teeming with life in summer, were bare and silent.

"There's something I want to ask you, Jenny," Robert said abruptly. "Would you mind very much if I married Sheila?"

Jenny's sharp intake of breath nearly froze her lungs to her ribcage. "Um, I don't know," she gasped. "I mean, I like Sheila, and she's a brilliant cook, but, but," her words trailed off.

"But?"

"But you can't love her as much as you loved Mum!" Jenny blurted out awkwardly.

"Oh, Jenny! Love isn't something you can measure like

that! I'll always love Mum in a very special way, but I really do love Sheila too – in a different special way."

"I-I just don't think it's right, Dad. It, um, seems sort of like saying you've forgotten about Mum, even if you haven't. I mean, how can you still love Mum *and* love Sheila? It's impossible! Horrible!"

Robert sighed. "I thought you might feel like that. Please forget I ever said anything."

They walked home in silence.

On Christmas Day everyone on Lundy had a buffet lunch in the Tavern, in front of a roaring, spitting driftwood fire. The Tavern was a haven of warmth and good cheer.

Jenny spent most of Christmas lunch feeling awkward, or wretched, or both. The Bonhams had arrived on Christmas Eve, and it was confusing seeing Hector again after the stamp incident and the exchange of several long letters. Jenny felt she'd got to know a different, much more likable, Hector through his letters. It had been much simpler to hate him.

She tried to avoid Sheila, but she was everywhere – cheerfully beavering away while everyone else enjoyed themselves. She seemed blissfully unaware that Jenny had ruined her life.

As soon as she could, Jenny slipped out of the Tavern. The north-easterly wind immediately sucked the warmth out of her. She went home for gloves, a hat and an extra coat, and then went to see the ponies. She'd helped her father feed them hay near the Quarter Wall that morning, so she knew they wouldn't be far away.

The freezing wind had turned the soil to rock, fossilising hoofprints and tractor-ruts. Small white specks of ice floated through the air and dusted the barren ground. Summer was a forgotten dream.

Everything's changed, Jenny thought as she approached the ponies. Even the ponies aren't the same, with no Midnight. The older mares have gone, too, including dear old Rosie.

The new stallion didn't fit in at all. He was a tall, thin, neurotic creature, and he chivvied the mares constantly. They all looked thoroughly fed up.

Only Gale seemed to be as good-natured as ever. She gave a high-pitched whinny, and trotted over. Her thick winter coat was a rich creamy colour, and her legs, mane and tail were dark. Her muzzle and the rims to her eyes were also dark, as if she'd skilfully applied makeup to highlight her lips and her large blue eyes.

"Oh! You're so beautiful!" Jenny whispered, stroking her and feeling a familiar ache of longing. Not just for ownership - Midnight had taught her that ownership by itself meant very little. More than anything else, she longed for - how could she describe it? True friendship? A special bond? She'd so nearly had it with Midnight, and then she'd destroyed it forever. With Gale it would be different. She'd get it right with Gale.

"Hello. Taking a break from all the festivities? One can't stay in the Tavern from dawn 'til dusk, can one? Even on Christmas Day."

Jenny jumped. "Mr Bonham! You gave me a shock!"

"I'm so sorry, I didn't mean to," he said. "That's the one you rescued - Gale, isn't it?"

"Yes. Isn't she lovely?"

"She certainly is. Incredibly tame, too. You seem to have struck up a great friendship."

"Yes. I was afraid she'd forget me while I was at school, but I don't think she has."

"Definitely not. She's obviously extremely fond of you - and you of her. Would you like her? I mean, I'd like to give her to you, as a thank you, a Christmas present."

Jenny's mouth gaped in disbelief. "As a what? Why?" she said, feeling her cheeks burn as she realised how stupid and ungrateful it sounded. "Sorry, I mean, um..."

Mr Bonham smiled. "No, I'm the one who should be sorry. It was stupid of me to spring it on you like that. You see, I really am extremely grateful to you for warning us all about Mr Wagstaff. Er, as I'm sure you realise, this place requires a great deal of money to keep it afloat, so to speak. Well, Mr Wagstaff came to me with a business proposition which seemed to solve a lot of problems. He's a very clever, persuasive man." He nodded towards the stallion. "He even persuaded me I needed that thing to improve the quality of the ponies, and what a mistake that's been! Anyway, I can assure you I had no idea about his secret plans to quarry Lundy. It would have ruined the place forever. However, thanks to you, we found out before it was too late. Your father tells me you've been learning to ride at school, and that you'd love to have your own pony to ride here, so it seemed to me that giving you Gale would be a good way of saying thank you."

Jenny stared at the piece of mane she'd unconsciously wound round her finger. Dark and light threads of hair entwined. She was Gale's owner, right down to her last hair. Just like that. Unbelievable.

Gale stood contentedly, enjoying the attention, with no idea of what ownership was or why it should matter to her.

"If you'd like her, of course. Your father said he thought you would," Mr Bonham added, with a hint of concern.

Jenny had to say something, however inadequate. "I'd love her," she said. "Thank you so, so much!"

When Jenny got home, her father was sitting at the kitchen table, drinking a cup of tea. Before him, untouched, was a Christmas cake; a present from Sheila, made with loving care. He looked up and tried to smile. "Cup of tea?" he asked.

"Yes please," said Jenny. She sat down beside him, and told him about Gale.

It was obvious he knew already, but he tried his best to act surprised.

"Oh, Dad! I'm so sorry about what I said yesterday," Jenny said finally. "You see, I've been thinking; I love Midnight, but I also love Gale, and owning Gale doesn't mean I love Midnight any less. They're different, and I love them both in different ways. Love isn't just one cake which has to be sliced up, is it? It's lots of different cakes for different people, or ponies, or whatever you happen to love. Um, I suppose what I'm trying to say is it's okay if you want to marry Sheila. I mean, please marry Sheila. I'd like you to marry her – really, I would."

The traditional Christmas dinner in the dining room of the Hotel that evening turned into an engagement party, which turned into a party in the Tavern. Jenny couldn't remember ever seeing her father so happy.

Jenny tried not to mind when he took Sheila in his arms and kissed her in front of everyone. She tried not to mind when he talked about the three of them being a family. It was hard, but she tried not to mind. She longed for Ben, and Midnight, and Lundy as it had been last summer – that wonderful time before her world had changed forever.

CHAPTER NINETEEN

After Christmas the weather became even colder. Jenny found a dead swan near Pondsbury, and thousands of other birds appeared: starlings, skylarks, song thrushes, snipe, lapwings, curlews and woodcock amongst them. All were weak with cold, starvation and thirst. They lay dying in the shelter of the farm buildings and walls, or were killed and eaten by the rats and black-backed gulls.

Jenny set up a makeshift bird hospital. She lined wooden boxes with wool and hay, and tried to feed the birds with strips of rabbit meat. She knew it was futile, but she had to do something.

The ponies were her main worry. Every day Jenny helped her father feed them hay, then break the thickening ice on Quarter Wall pond with a crowbar, and every day she noticed they looked thinner and moved around less.

On New Year's Eve it snowed properly for the first time, and she could stand it no longer. She persuaded her father to let her keep Gale and Kit in a spare shed in the farmyard. The weedy stallion was also housed, but in a separate shed, and Jenny made him a rug out of hessian sacks. As she got to know him better she felt sorry for him. He was born to be a cosseted show animal, not a herd stallion fending for himself on a windswept island. It wasn't his fault he was useless; he'd been given the wrong job.

The only good thing about the cold weather, as far as Jenny was concerned, was that there was the distinct possibility she wouldn't be able to get back to school in time for the beginning of term. The boat was iced-in on the mainland, and two sailings had been cancelled already.

The other islanders were anxious. Supplies were running short, and there had been no mail since Christmas Eve.

Unfortunately for Jenny – or fortunately, as it turned out – Mr Bonham was very eager to get himself back to London and his children back to school, so he managed to persuade the skipper of a boat from Wales to take his family and Jenny to Swansea early one morning, from where they caught trains to their various destinations.

It had been arranged, via the Coastguard at Hartland, that Jenny would stay with the Scoines family in Appledore for the night, even though Albert was on Lundy.

As she sat on the train, Jenny thought about seeing Ben again, and felt all tingly.

At last, after a complicated train journey involving changes at Bristol and Taunton, Jenny arrived at Barnstaple Junction at three o'clock in the afternoon. Now she had to find the bus station, and catch the bus to Appledore.

She picked up her overnight-case, and started making her way along the platform to the exit.

"Jenny! Over here!" It was Ben! His fair hair bobbed above the sea of heads as he jumped up and down, waving his arms, then weaved through the crowd to meet her.

"Hello, stranger," he said, reaching for her suitcase. "I'll take that, if you like." He pretended to drop the case as soon as he took it. "Crikey! What have you got in here? Bricks?"

Jenny giggled. "Edible bricks," she said. "Sheila made masses of fudge for me to take back to school."

"Mmm, I might just have to confiscate some of that in payment for your taxi."

Jenny was amazed. "What, you took a taxi all the way from Appledore? That must have cost a fortune!"

They were outside now, and the cold air nearly took Jenny's breath away after the fuggy warmth of the train.

"Twenty pounds," said Ben, reaching in his pocket and pulling out some keys.

"*Twenty pounds!*" Jenny echoed.

"Yes. You can't really buy a decent second-hand car for less than that nowadays," Ben said, unlocking the door of a bottle green Morris 1000 van. He held the door open, and saluted. "Your taxi awaits, ma'am."

"Wow! Is this really yours?" Jenny exclaimed, settling into the well-worn passenger seat. "When did you pass your test?"

"As soon as I could after my seventeenth birthday."

"Oh, when were you seventeen?" Jenny asked, feeling guilty she'd missed it.

Ben went round the other side, got into the driver's seat and started the engine. "November. And I passed my test just before Christmas. Not bad, eh?"

Jenny was sure Mrs Hamilton wouldn't really approve of Ben giving her a lift to Appledore in his car. And *what* would Miss Nash say? The thought made an already thrilling experience even better.

"What news from Lundy?" Ben asked, manoeuvring his car out into the traffic.

"Golly, where do I begin?" Jenny replied, and told him about the engagement, Gale, the useless stallion and the poor frozen birds.

Gradually the houses of Barnstaple gave way to fields, and the tarmac became covered with hard-packed snow.

"I'd better put on some snow chains," Ben said, pulling

up by the side of the road. "You stay here. It won't take long." Expertly, he laid some chains down, drove over them and fixed them in place.

Jenny felt in awe. He seemed so grown-up and capable all of a sudden. She hardly dared ask the question which had been burning in her mind ever since they'd left the station, but she had to before it became too late. "Can we go and see Midnight? I haven't seen him for ages, and I'm a bit worried about him, with the snow and everything."

"Okay. Good idea. I looked in on him last week, and he seemed fine. I suppose if he can survive on Lundy, he can survive anywhere."

Jenny wondered why she'd worried about asking. She chatted away as the colourless winter landscape rolled by. The countryside looked like a massive Christmas cake covered in snowy icing, with trees and hedges for decoration. There were twenty-four hours of freedom before the beginning of term. She'd savour every minute: riding in Ben's car, going to see Midnight and sleeping in the cosy little attic room in Appledore, with Ben's room just below. She felt blissfully happy.

Before long they were driving cautiously along the narrow lane to Midnight's field, following some deep, bumpy ruts in the frozen snow which looked as if they'd been forged by a tractor. Steep snow drifts rose up on either side, like white hedges.

A scraping noise came from underneath the car, and it ground to a halt.

Ben swore. "I knew we should have walked down," he said. "We've had a lot of snow since I came down last week." He put the car into reverse. The engine revved, but they didn't move. He swore again. "We'll have to walk."

Slipping occasionally, they picked their way down the icy lane to Midnight's field. The air felt viciously cold.

Jenny had been far too hot on the train, but now she was glad Mrs Hamilton had insisted on her wearing a woollen vest and Long Johns under her trousers and jumper for the boat journey, together with a hat, gloves, thick socks and a padded anorak.

Midnight's field came into view. Jenny could see him there, standing near the gate. She walked faster.

"Mid-night!" she called as they got closer. "Hello boy! I've missed you."

Midnight stood, looking at her.

She ran ahead of Ben, slithering and tripping.

"Guess what? I've been to Lundy! I've got lots to tell you," she said breathlessly.

Midnight stood still.

She navigated her way through the hay-covered snow by the entrance to the field, which had been churned up and was littered with frozen cowpats. "Hello, old boy. It's me, Jenny. Remember?" She climbed over the gate, slipping on the iced rungs. All the time she watched Midnight, waiting for his reaction.

He just stood there, eyes half-closed, ears almost pricked, one hind foot resting. Peaceful. Much too peaceful.

Jenny felt her insides contracting with fear as she hurried towards him. "Midnight?" she said. "Midnight!" She touched his neck.

It felt stone-cold. His coat was spiky, as if it had been sweaty and had then frozen.

"Midnight! No! No! Oh, *please no!*" she wailed, searching frantically for any signs of life. Nothing.

Ben was beside her now. She felt his hand on her shoulder. "I'm so sorry, Jenny! I had no idea. How awful!" There was a pause, and then he said, "I wonder where the cattle are. They must have been moved out, judging by all that mess around the gate. By the looks of it, he's been tramping up and down this hedge for ages; look at that deep track he's made. And the pile of hay over there hasn't been touched. How peculiar."

"He - hates - being - alone," Jenny managed to say between sobs. "I expect - t-that's - why - he - d-decided to d-die." She hugged his prickly neck and buried her face in his thick mane.

"Look! Did you see that?" Ben said. "His eyelid moved! I'm sure it did!"

Willing Ben to be right, Jenny studied Midnight's deep blue eyes. They seemed to flicker with life, like the dying embers of a fire. Am I imagining it? She thought.

By way of an answer, Midnight blinked.

"He's alive!" she screamed. "Oh, Ben! He's alive!"

"You stay with him, and I'll go to Home Farm for help," Ben said, and disappeared.

A few minutes later, he returned carrying Jenny's suitcase and a dusty tartan rug. "Me again! I thought these might come in handy." He smiled. "Particularly the fudge."

"Thanks," Jenny said, taking the rug from him so she could put it on Midnight. "Take some fudge with you, if you like."

Ben opened the suitcase, revealing an old biscuit tin, a sponge bag and some slippers. They looked rather surreal, lying there in the snow. He pulled out the tin, and opened the lid. "Thank goodness for Sheila," he said, offering the tin to Jenny.

She took a couple of pieces of fudge, and ate one. It was hard, sugary and chocolate-flavoured.

Ben stuffed some into his mouth. "Yum! I really *am* going to Home Farm now," he mumbled. "I'll be as quick as I can."

Jenny bit off a small piece of fudge and pushed it into

Midnight's cold, rubbery mouth. She carried on, a tiny piece at a time, until his mouth was a sticky mess.

His tongue moved slightly, and he attempted to swallow.

The night was drawing in fast, dragging the temperature even lower.

Jenny looked up at the clear sky. A new moon, sharp as an icicle, shone down. Out of habit, she found the Plough, then Leo and then Regulus, the lion's heart. It gave her courage. Although her hands ached with cold, she carried on trying to feed Midnight and gently rubbing his rigid body over the tartan blanket she'd draped over his back. It seemed hopeless – like feeding the birds in the bird hospital – but she refused to give up.

Snow smothered her feet, and seeped through her leather lace-up shoes. She felt like crying out with the pain. Somehow, she had to get her feet dry before they froze.

It must be worth a try, she thought. She took a spare pair of socks and her slippers from her suitcase, closed it, wedged it upright in some snow, and then stood on it. Leaning against Midnight for support, she took off her wet shoes and socks and, with difficulty, put on the dry socks and slippers. Then, with all her remaining strength, she grabbed a handful of mane and clambered onto Midnight's back, taking care not to dislodge the tartan blanket.

For a moment she was on Lundy, sitting on Midnight. She could smell the air, and hear the seabirds calling.

"Please live," she whispered. "I'll take you back there. I'll take you back to Lundy." She leant forward and hugged his solid neck, trying to give him whatever warmth she had left in her shivering body.

Darkness fell. The cold sapped her senses, dulling her will to keep going, but she lay there, clinging to Midnight's neck, although her whole body felt numb.

It occurred to Jenny that she and Midnight might both freeze before Ben returned. They'd be found frozen together. Rather poetic, really, she thought hazily, and a warm feeling came over her. *I have become responsible, forever, for what I have tamed....*

CHAPTER TWENTY

"She's coming round, Sister."

I haven't got a sister, Jenny thought. This has to be the weirdest, most horrible dream. My throat feels like sandpaper, and something's strapped over my mouth. Everything hurts. Best to go back to sleep...

"Jenny? Can you hear me? You're in hospital, dear," said a kind voice. "You were very cold, but you're warming up again now. No, don't rip off your oxygen mask, there's a good girl. Try to keep still, now. Just relax."

Easy for you to say, Jenny thought. Your body doesn't feel as if it's being stabbed by hundreds of tiny pins, your eyes aren't glued shut and your head doesn't feel as if it will split open. Sleep...

"Don't go back to sleep, dear. Wake up, now. There's a nice warm drink here for you."

Leave me alone! Jenny thought, or did she shout it? She wasn't sure.

They wouldn't leave her alone. They made her wake up. It was so hard, like wading through treacle. Why couldn't she sleep? She wanted to sleep so badly.

"Just small sips, dear. It's a warm chocolate drink. I bet that tastes good!"

Jenny couldn't taste anything at all. Her tongue wouldn't work properly. She dribbled. The drink blazed a path down her raw throat.

They bathed her eyes with warm water, and she managed to open them. Everything looked fuzzy. Briefly she took in the hospital ward, the nurses, and all the equipment round her. There were tubes coming out of her, or going in? She wasn't sure – too much effort to think.

At last, they allowed her to go back to sleep.

When Jenny woke again, she'd recovered enough to worry. "How's Midnight?" she whispered hoarsely to the nurse on duty.

"No, about six o'clock. It'll be breakfast time in a minute," the nurse replied.

It took a while for Jenny to work out what the nurse was talking about.

"I mean my pony!" Jenny whispered, exasperated that her throat wouldn't let her talk properly. "My pony's called Midnight. Is he okay?"

"I'm sure he is," said the nurse, with a reassuring smile. "Now then, let's take your temperature and see how your blood pressure's doing, shall we?"

Jenny didn't feel at all reassured. She asked everyone who came into the ward about Midnight, but nobody seemed to know anything. Nobody realised how important it was. Nobody cared.

The morning dragged on. Jenny slept and worried, worried and slept.

After lunch the morning shift left, and some new nurses appeared. Jenny wasted no time in asking them about Midnight. Again, they were pleasant but unhelpful. One, however, was younger and more talkative than the others.

"I'm sorry, love. I'm not at all horsey, so I wouldn't know," the nurse said. She plumped up Jenny's pillows as she talked, to make it look as if she were doing something useful. "They're nasty, dangerous things, if you ask me. The girl I share a room with works in the Emergency Ward, and she says more people are hurt by horses than by anything else. Only this morning she was telling me about a young man they had to patch up yesterday. In a very bad way, he was. She had to work right through her lunch break, so she was proper starving by tea time. Apparently he'd been attacked by a mad horse somewhere down on the marshes. People shouldn't be allowed to keep dangerous animals like that, if you want my opinion."

Jenny didn't want the nurse's opinion, mainly because she had a sneaking suspicion it applied to her, but she was intrigued by the information. She tried to make her throbbing brain concentrate. As far as she knew, Midnight was the most likely candidate for the title of 'mad horse somewhere down on the marshes'. Had Midnight attacked somebody yesterday morning? If so, why?

"Um, is the young man still here, in the hospital?" she asked.

"Oh, I expect so. By the sounds of it, he'll be here for some time."

"Can you find out who he is, and which ward he's in?"

The nurse hesitated. "I suppose so. Why?"

"I think I know him," Jenny said. Well, it could be true, couldn't it? she thought.

A young man Jenny really did know turned up at visiting time that evening.

Just when Jenny thought everyone out there in the real world had forgotten about her, Ben and Ada Scoines came hurrying in. Ben walked with a limp, and he looked tired.

"That blooming pony of yours!" he said.

"How is he?" Jenny asked, hardly daring to listen to the reply.

"He's okay. Tough as old boots," Ben replied. "They wanted to put him down there and then, in the field, but for some reason I persuaded them to give him a chance."

"Oh, thank goodness for that! Thank you! Where is he now?"

"Back at Home Farm."

"How on earth did you get him back there?"

"Well, by the time we arrived back at the field, Midnight was coming round a bit. He'd walked over to the gate, with you lying on his back. Do you remember?"

"No. I remember getting onto his back, but I don't remember much after that. How incredible I didn't fall off!"

"Your arms were locked so tightly round his neck that we had a job prising you away from him. He wasn't happy about us taking you away, either. He became very agitated."

"Did he?" Jenny said eagerly. "What did he do?"

"He bit me, amongst other things. Look." Ben rolled up his sleeve, to reveal a nasty bruise. Anyway, we managed to drive him into the horsebox, step by step, and we took him back to a stable at Home Farm. He came round quite quickly after that, with the help of a warm bran mash and lots of blankets. I made the mistake of staying with him in the stable, though."

"Why? What happened?" Jenny asked, hoping the young nurse with strong opinions about dangerous horses wasn't listening.

"As he thawed out, he went completely mad. I had to hide in the hay rack, and wait for him to go to sleep. I was there for ages, freezing to death, and then I sprained my ankle getting down again – blooming thing!"

Jenny was glad to see that Ben was smiling. He obviously thought the whole thing was a huge adventure really.

"Anyway, you'll never guess what!" Ben continued. "Those cattle which were in the field with Midnight must have been st..."

"Ah, Jennifer!"

With impeccably bad timing, Miss Nash breezed in, stopping Ben mid-sentence. Jenny willed him to continue, but he just smiled charmingly at Miss Nash, and offered her his chair.

"How are you, Jennifer?" Miss Nash asked, rudely ignoring Ben and his mother.

Jenny felt like saying, "Much better, until you came in." She said, "Much better, thank you, Miss Nash. Um, have you met Mrs Scoines and Ben Scoines? They're the people I stayed with at half term."

"*With whom I stayed*," Miss Nash corrected automatically, looking disapprovingly over her glasses.

Please go away, Jenny thought.

Miss Nash didn't. She stayed, and talked about her trials and tribulations at St Anne's: frozen pipes, no water, ice-bound lacrosse pitches and snow-bound staff and pupils. On account of the difficulties arising from the extreme weather conditions, the decision had been made that morning to postpone the beginning of term for at least a week. But, she said, with an air of martyrdom, despite all the problems, she'd made arrangements for Jenny to have a room in the Sick Bay after she left hospital.

Jenny listened, appalled by the prospect of solitary confinement in a freezing cold Sick Bay, nursed by Miss Nash.

"She can stay with us, if she likes," Ada said in her gentle North Devon accent.

Miss Nash stared at her with cool superiority. "Thank you, but that won't be necessary," she replied, pronouncing every word in her clipped, over-polished manner.

"Oh please may I?" Jenny blurted out, her voice still husky. "I mean, I'm terribly grateful to you but, with all the problems at school to sort out, looking after me is the last thing you need, Miss Nash."

Miss Nash looked doubtful.

"She'll be no problem," Ada cut in quickly. "Our cottage is warm, and I'll take good care of her. I can ask her father through the Hartland Coastguard tomorrow morning, if you like."

"Very well, then. If you're sure, Mrs, er, Mrs..."

"Scoines. Ada Scoines."

Miss Nash gave the briefest of smiles. "Very well, Mrs Scoines. I'm very grateful to you."

Ada and Miss Nash went to find the Ward Sister, leaving Jenny a few precious minutes with Ben before the end of visiting time.

"You've got the best mum in the whole world!" Jenny said.

"I've trained her well, haven't I?" Ben said. "Listen, those cattle in Midnight's field must have been stolen sometime between when Mr Moat fed them at about eleven in the morning and when we got there at around four in the afternoon!"

"Gosh! That's why Midnight had frozen sweat all over him, and why he'd been pacing up and down!" Jenny exclaimed. "The new hay in the field hadn't been touched, had it? So the cattle must have been taken soon after they were fed."

"Elementary, my dear Watson!" Ben teased.

"But why did they leave Midnight?" Jenny wondered out loud.

In answer, Ben rolled up his sleeve to reveal the bite mark. "Perhaps he didn't give a good impression."

"Oh, very funny!" Jenny said. Everything was falling into place. "Ben, I think one of the thieves is somewhere in this hospital."

"What on earth..."

"You see, that nurse over there told me a young man was taken to the Emergency Ward yesterday lunch-time because he'd been attacked by a mad horse somewhere down on the marshes. It's too much of a coincidence, isn't it?"

"Jenny, you're a genius!" Ben declared, patting her hand. "I'd better go and tell the police. I'll come and get you tomorrow, all being well. Okay?"

"Very okay," Jenny said. Exhausted, but happy, she sank back against the pillows.

CHAPTER TWENTY-ONE

True to his word, Ben collected Jenny from hospital the following afternoon, and took her back to Appledore and the cosy attic bedroom she almost thought of as her own. Warm, undisturbed and truly comfortable at last, she spent the next couple of days sleeping and eating. Every evening she waited eagerly for Ben to come home from work with an update on Midnight's recovery and the police investigation into the robbery.

The news from the police was good. The cattle thieves had been caught, thanks to Jenny's tip-off, and the steers had been returned to Home Farm. Ben said that Mr Moat was delighted, and very grateful.

Midnight was obviously feeling much better, and was becoming a nuisance. Ben said he was driving everyone mad, whinnying and kicking the stable all the time – especially when he saw another horse, which was often.

"It's Saturday tomorrow, so I can take you over to Home Farm in my car, if you feel up to it," Ben said on the third evening. "Then you can see Midnight."

"Thanks. I'd love that," Jenny said.

Fresh snow fell that night, obliterating previous efforts to clear doorsteps, pavements and roads so that normal life could carry on.

For a terrible moment Jenny thought Ben would say he couldn't take her to Home Farm because of the weather, but she needn't have worried.

"I like a challenge," he said, as they forged a path through the white expanse which had once been a road, guessing where the verge stopped and the tarmac began. "I think I'll park on the top road, though, and we'll have to walk the last bit. I don't want to get stuck again."

The stable yard was deserted when they arrived, but fresh footprints criss-crossed in the snow.

Jenny felt glad Ben was there, and no one else. Only Ben understood the importance of the moment.

One loose box had a bar across the top door. The horse inside whinnied.

"Midnight! Hello!" Jenny called, hurrying over.

Midnight whinnied urgently, and pawed at the door. His muzzle appeared over the top of the bar, then disappeared as he paced round the stable, then appeared again over the bar, whiskers quivering and nostrils wide with excitement.

"He recognises you," Ben said. "Most people don't get that sort of welcome."

"Why is there a bar across the door?" Jenny asked.

"To stop him from jumping out. I think it's also supposed to stop him from pawing at the door, but it doesn't seem to."

Jenny reached the stable and put the back of her hand up to stroke Midnight's nose, ready to snatch it away if he tried to bite.

He didn't try to bite. He sniffed her hand, then licked it, then gave a soft murmur of recognition.

He does recognise me! He really does! He knows it's me! He *likes* me! Jenny thought, feeling light-headed with elation. Without a second thought she unbolted the stable door and went in.

"Jenny, do be careful!" she heard Ben say.

He needn't have worried. Midnight greeted her with a low, affectionate mumble.

She stroked him and talked to him. Then, sure at last that she'd regained his trust, she wrapped her arms round his neck, drinking in the old familiar smell of his warm body. He loves me again, she thought. If it's possible to burst with happiness, I think I just might.

People had arrived in the yard. Jenny could hear voices. She clung on to Midnight, not wanting the feeling to end.

The voices came nearer.

Ben's voice said, "She's over there in the stable with him."

"Good Lord! Is she all right?" Mrs Moat's voice.

"Yes, they're both fine. Take a look."

Midnight shifted uneasily, and Jenny knew somebody was looking over the door.

"Well, I can see you've found a friend! How about a cup of tea?" Mrs Moat said.

Reluctantly, Jenny left Midnight's stable and followed Mrs Moat and Ben into the farmhouse.

Mrs Moat's kitchen was just as Jenny thought a farmhouse kitchen should be – clean enough, but homely, with a large wooden kitchen table and a huge cream-coloured Aga. A couple of dogs got up from their baskets to greet them. The cat sleeping by the Aga didn't move.

"How are you, Jenny?" Mrs Moat asked, pouring out the tea.

"Much better, thank you, especially now I've seen Midnight. He really seems to like people again, doesn't he?"

"Well, he likes you, anyway, and he doesn't mind me. He wasn't too keen on you, though, was he, Ben? And he tried to bite my husband yesterday. Horses which have been treated badly by men often end up hating all men, but tolerating women. Some just hate everybody, and will only trust a few chosen people. If a horse has been badly treated, you really have to earn its friendship."

"How?" Jenny asked.

Mrs Moat smiled. "You tell me! You've won over Midnight. I bet he knows how much you wanted him to live. He realises you truly love him."

"But I've always loved him!" Jenny protested.

Mrs Moat sipped her tea. "Ah, but horses are simple creatures," she said. "By simple I mean straightforward, not stupid. Humans are much more complicated. Humans often want to do one thing but actually do something completely different, for one reason or another. To a horse, that's a lie. Horses never lie, and they don't understand it when we do – even if we've done so with the best of intentions."

Jenny sighed. "I know."

Even though they were in the kitchen, they could hear Midnight whinnying and banging his stable door.

"One thing's for certain," said Mrs Moat. "He can't stay in that stable much longer, or we'll all go mad. He tries to attack geldings, and he's a terrible flirt with the mares. Even my staid old mares have become skittish with him around. No, the only place we can keep him is in the same field as before, with his old friends the steers for company. Of course, we'll padlock the gate this time, and we'll keep a careful watch on them all while the weather's bad. Anyway, he's welcome to stay there until April, Jenny, but then I'm afraid the steers will be sold and the field laid up for hay, so there'll be nowhere for him to go after that. Have you made any headway with finding somewhere else?"

Jenny stared blankly at her mug of tea. She didn't know what to say. How could she have been so stupid? While he'd been tucked away in the field with the steers, she'd conveniently forgotten the fact that the arrangement was temporary. What on earth was she going to do? "Not yet," she said, still staring at the mug. "But I've got one or two ideas."

"Good," said Mrs Moat, getting up from the table. The dogs instantly came over, tails wagging. "Well, you've got plenty of time to sort out something - nearly three months."

Jenny knew that nearly three months wasn't plenty of time, especially when most of it was going to be spent imprisoned at school.

"Have you really got one or two ideas?" Ben asked as they drove back to Appledore.

The road had lots of tyre marks along it now, and most of the snow had been squashed into ice.

"Not really. Well, perhaps one."

"Where?"

"Lundy."

"*What?*"

"Lundy. You see, I promised him."

"Promised who?"

"Midnight. I promised Midnight I'd take him back to Lundy, so I've got to, haven't I? He belongs there. I owe it to him."

"Blimey! How are you going to manage that?"

"With difficulty."

"You can say that again!"

"With difficulty!" Jenny shouted.

Ben winced. "It's okay, I heard you the first time."

That night Jenny sat up in the little attic room, composing a letter to Mr Bonham. By morning she had a full waste paper basket, a splitting headache and a letter to post. She read the letter through one more time.

Dear Mr Bonham,

I hope you are well. I was very cold (they call it hypothermia) but I am better now. Midnight was very cold too, but he is also better now. He attacked some thieves who stole the cattle which share his field, and the thieves were caught. The other good news is he likes me again.

The reason why I am writing is that I want to ask you a huge favour. I hope you don't mind, but I have got to ask it for Midnight's sake. I promised him I would.

Please will you let Midnight come back to Lundy?

I have been thinking a lot about this, and I realise it is a lot to ask, so if you like I'll give back Gale and have Midnight on Lundy as my present for finding out about Mr Wagstaff. Gale doesn't need me, but Midnight does, although I love them both very much. I feel responsible for Midnight. He has been through such a lot, and most of it is my fault. I need to put things right. He loves Lundy, and he belongs there, like we do.

Midnight is used to living in a field now, so I am sure he would be happy in a field with one or two of the older mares (not his daughters) for company. I will work as hard as I can to pay for his keep.

He has got to leave Home Farm in April, because they are selling the cattle and using the field for hay.

I am staying with the Scoines family in Appledore at the moment, which is nice. School is supposed to be starting next week, so please could you send your reply to St Anne's School, Bideford, North Devon.

Thank you very much.

Yours sincerely
Jenny Medway

Jenny wasn't sure about 'Yours sincerely'. It looked so stuffy and formal. She wrote the letter out again, with 'Love from' at the end, but that sounded cheeky. How about 'From'? She wrote the whole thing out again. No, it sounded as if she didn't care. She'd have to go for 'Yours sincerely', and hope for the best.

The next day Ben drove her over to Home Farm again. The air had become warmer, turning the snow slushy on top but making little impression on the hard-packed ice underneath. They slithered on foot down the lane to the stables.

Midnight greeted them with frantic whinnying and door-banging.

"Oh, do shut up, Midnight!" Mrs Moat shouted, poking her head out of the tack room door. She spotted Jenny and Ben. "Jolly good! I hoped you'd come. I've got a job for you!" She dived back into the tack room, and came out with a headcollar. "Here we are. You can lead Midnight back to the field. I don't know who'll be more relieved: he or I. The steers are already down there, and Fred put some hay there earlier." She rummaged in her pocket. "Oh, and here's the key for the padlock. What a blooming nuisance it is, having to lock everything!"

Somehow, Jenny and Ben managed to get Midnight back to the field. They tried in vain to lead him. Instead, he hauled them, skidding behind him, for most of the way.

Jenny was incredibly relieved when they eventually arrived in the field. She undid the buckle of Midnight's headcollar, and he instantly pulled away and went charging over to the steers, scattering them in a flurry of snow. Then, with a blissful groan, he sank into the snow, and rolled, over and back, and over again.

Jenny watched, revelling in the moment with him, feeling the cool balm of the snow on his itchy, dusty, stable-weary body. She, too, felt hot and prickly after their manic walk.

"I bet that feels good," Ben said, reading her mind. "I'm tempted to go and join him."

Instead, Midnight got up, gave a joyous buck, and came trotting over to them. He stopped in front of Jenny, touched her hand lightly with his muzzle, and then trotted off to his field-mates.

"He just said thank you! I'm sure he did!" Jenny said.

CHAPTER TWENTY-TWO

For once everything went right – at least, everything to do with Midnight. School was much the same, but the bullying and pettiness didn't worry Jenny anymore. She was too busy counting the days, hours and minutes until the Easter holidays.

Every day she took the letter out of her locker and read it again, just to make sure:

My Dear Jenny,

Thank you very much for your letter. Of course Midnight must come back to Lundy. It would be sensible for you to travel with him at the beginning of the Easter holidays, if it can be arranged. I will contact Captain Dover and see what can be done.

Your idea of a field for Midnight with a couple of the older mares for company is an excellent one. I trust you will train him to recognise the difference between thieves and day-trippers!

Gale is still yours, and I hope you will gain as much enjoyment from her as your mother did from her Lundy pony, Puffin.

I look forward to seeing you, and Midnight, on Lundy at Easter. As you so rightly say, it's where we all belong.

Yours sincerely,
Jeremy Bonham

PS I expect your friend, Frances Knighton, has told you already that she and her family will be my guests at Millcombe over Easter. Mrs Hamilton arranged for me to meet the Knightons in London just before Christmas, and I must say I liked them enormously. John Knighton has been very helpful, and I think he will prove to be a great friend to Lundy.

Midnight was going back to Lundy! He'd be able to live out his old age at home, where he belonged. She'd be able to keep her promise to him. The icing on the cake was that Fran would be on Lundy for Easter as well.

Whenever she could, Jenny went to see Midnight in his field. Seeing him had become a pleasure once more. The bond they'd once had seemed even stronger now. He always whinnied and trotted over when he saw her, and he'd follow her around the field without a headcollar. Jenny hoped the strength of his trust in her would overcome his fear of the boat journey. She prepared him as well as she could in the field, teaching him to lead properly, and to accept the feeling of ropes and straps round his body.

Captain Dover had been persuaded, somehow, by Mr Bonham to provide a special trip for Jenny and Midnight on the day Jenny broke up from school. Mrs Moat had agreed to transport Midnight down to Bideford Quay in her horse lorry. Albert, who would be home on leave, had agreed to pick up Jenny and her luggage from school. She would leave early, missing the final school assembly of term – a special concession granted by Miss Nash, but only after the intervention of Mr Bonham. It appeared even Miss Nash wasn't immune to his charming good manners.

Everything which could possibly be organised had been. The only thing out of everybody's control was the weather. As the end of term approached, Jenny took a keen interest in the wind direction and the appearance of Lundy from the lax pitches. One of the first rhymes she'd been taught by her mother had been:

Lundy high, it will be dry.
Lundy low, it will be snow.
Lundy plain, it will be rain.
Lundy in haze, fine for days.

It hadn't made much sense when she was living on Lundy, but now it did. Jenny hoped it was accurate, because Lundy looked hazy for a couple of days before the end of term.

On the last night Jenny hardly slept at all. At a quarter-past-five in the morning she went to the loo with her radio, tuned it to the BBC Light Programme and listened intently for the final verdict on the weather in store.

'*....Lundy, Fastnet, Irish Sea: south or southwest one or two, occasionally three in Irish Sea. Slight. Mainly fair. Moderate or good....*'

Better than she'd dared hope for! Now all she had to do was wait, counting the minutes until Albert picked her up at nine o'clock.

She couldn't eat any breakfast. She didn't even want to join in with the end-of-term chatter. The day she'd been longing for had finally arrived. She felt trapped in a bubble of anxiety, suspended in time and place, unable to cope with the magnitude of what lay ahead.

Albert arrived at nine o'clock on the dot.

In a daze, Jenny greeted him, loaded her luggage into his car, gave Fran and some other friends a farewell hug and settled into the front seat. As they drove away, Jenny felt as if she were playing a part in some film or other. This couldn't really be happening, could it? She couldn't be on her way to Bideford Quay, to take Midnight back to Lundy!

Albert told her about Robert and Sheila moving into Stoneycroft, by the Old Light, and said they seemed very happy there.

Jenny knew about the move from her father's letters. He'd been so enthusiastic about it, saying there'd be much more space inside and a lovely walled garden outside. He loved gardening.

She couldn't imagine living anywhere but Number One Barton Cottages. Besides, she'd planned to keep Midnight in St Helen's Field, right by the cottage. She doubted whether her father would let her keep any ponies in the Lighthouse Field, next to Stoneycroft – it was too valuable for lambing and haymaking. First I've got to get Midnight back to Lundy, then I'll start worrying about minor details like where I'm going to keep him, she thought.

Albert gave Jenny other news from Lundy. Gale and Kit were fine, and had become very tame. Lambing had been a disaster, because the sheep were so weak after the harsh winter. Batty's birthday party in the Tavern at the end of March had been a grand occasion, as usual, and Mrs Hamilton had excelled herself with a birthday cake which looked like Tibbett's, complete with rather off-putting granite icing, made by mixing burnt toast crumbs with icing sugar. There had been yet another landslip onto the Beach Road, and the first puffins and shearwaters had arrived....

Jenny wanted to listen, but she was too distracted to take in what he was saying. By the tone of Albert's voice, he was asking her a question. She tried to concentrate. "Sorry, what did you say?"

"Do you get the *North Devon Journal* at school?"

What an odd thing to ask, Jenny thought. "No, I don't think so."

"Ah, so you didn't see the article about Midnight, and all the readers' letters which followed?"

"No. What article?"

"Somehow they got hold of the story about Midnight attacking those thieves, and you saving him from freezing to death. Anyway, the article prompted lots of letters – some saying what a hero he is and some, I'm sorry to say, voicing the opinion that it's irresponsible to keep such a dangerous animal. The upshot is that Midnight's become quite a celebrity, and I'm afraid there may be several people down on the quay to see him loaded onto the boat, including members of the press."

Jenny was dumbstruck.

"I'm sorry. It must be the last thing you want to hear, but I thought I'd better warn you."

"Um, is Ben going to be there?"

"I don't know. He left the house before I had a chance to speak to him. I expect he's working."

"Oh."

Albert was right. People thronged the quayside, including a couple of policemen and several reporters with large cameras.

Albert parked the car, and turned to Jenny. "Are you okay? You needn't do this if you don't want to, you know," he said.

Jenny thought about her dream; the vision she'd played

over in her head so many times it had to come true – the vision of Midnight set free on Lundy. She'd rather die than turn back now. "No, I'm fine. Let's go," she said.

They eased through the crowd to the boat, and put Jenny's cases down on the quayside next to it. Jenny saw Captain Dover carrying the mail sack on board, and tried to catch his attention, but at that moment a large man and an equally large lady hurried towards them. The man looked like a fisherman. Jenny recognised him from somewhere.

"Albert! Hello, my old chum! And how are you, Jenny? Quite a crowd you've mustered, eh? I must introduce you to my little sister, Rose – the pony-mad one I was telling you about. She's a great admirer of your Midnight, you know."

Of course! Jenny thought as she shook the lady's hand. Bob's your uncle! Uncle Bob, who bought my stamps.

The large lady said that she'd bought two in-foal Lundy mares in the past which had given birth to lovely foals, both by Midnight. The foals had gone on to be brilliant jumping ponies with various people, and she was longing to see the famous Midnight in the flesh. She loved Lundy ponies, and had quite a collection of them, but she'd never been to Lundy. Wasn't it always the way? Places nearby always got overlooked when choosing a destination for a holiday. Mind you, being farmers, they very rarely went anywhere....

Jenny smiled and tried to make polite conversation, but she was too nervous to think straight. She couldn't even remember what the large lady was called, other than the unlikely label of 'little sister'.

"Well, we mustn't keep you, but I just need to have a quick word with Jenny, in private, if I may," said Uncle Bob. He put his hand on Jenny's shoulder, and steered her towards the suitcases on the quayside. Once there, he gave her the large envelope which he'd been carrying. "Your stamps," he said. "It was wrong of me to take them from you."

"But..."

"No buts. They're yours."

"But you didn't take them; you bought them for a lot of money, and there's no way I can pay you back!" Jenny protested. "I used the money to buy Midnight."

"I know. Don't worry about it. All in a good cause. I more or less stole them from you, anyway. I've since discovered they're worth much more than I gave you, so not another word. The money covered the pleasure I had in looking after them for a while. Now then, put them into your suitcase quickly, there's a good girl. It sounds as if your pony's arriving."

Jenny hastily said thank you, and did as she was told.

The police called, "Mind your backs, please! Make way!"

The crowd murmured, and shuffled out of the way as Mrs Moat's horse lorry drew up, halting with a shudder and a hiss of brakes.

Overjoyed, Jenny noticed Ben was in the passenger seat. He jumped down from the cab, grinning. "Hello, Jenny. I like the fan club - most impressive!"

Jenny laughed, and hugged him. Everything would be all right, now that Ben was there.

The lorry rocked slightly, and there was a banging noise as Midnight pawed at the partition.

Mrs Moat and Ben went round to lower the ramp, and Jenny hurried over to join them.

Jenny had never seen Mrs Moat look so rattled. She stood with her hand on the catch of the closed ramp. "I really think we ought to give up this idea altogether, Jenny," she said earnestly. Her voice shook with anxiety. "I've been around horses for long enough to know that this is an accident waiting to happen. It's just not safe, especially with all these people around. If Midnight broke free it could be disastrous. I'll tell you what, he can stay at Home Farm until you find him somewhere to live on the mainland, okay?"

Jenny looked at Mrs Moat, Ben, the lorry with Midnight inside, the boat, the settled grey sky and the calm grey water. Everything had been brought together for this moment. She'd been given the chance of a lifetime. She couldn't throw it away. "Thanks very much for the offer, but I really do want to take him back to Lundy. He'll be okay, I know he will," she said.

"I hope you're right," Mrs Moat said, and she and Ben lowered the heavy ramp.

The lorry rocked violently. Midnight whinnied loudly from inside.

The crowd became restless with anticipation.

Jenny walked up the ramp, calling Midnight's name.

He replied with an affectionate rumble.

Glancing at her audience, Jenny spotted a thin man in a tweed cap. Dobbin!

Midnight pawed at the floor of the lorry, impatient to be released.

Jenny opened up the side-gates, and squeezed through the partition so she could untie him. "There's a good boy. We'll show them what a good boy you are, especially mean old Mr Dobbin out there, eh?" Jenny whispered.

Midnight nuzzled her. He seemed remarkably calm, and none the worse for his journey so far.

"We can do it! I know we can," Jenny told him. "I'm taking you back to Lundy, Midnight, just like I promised. You'll be there by lunch time, and you'll never have to leave again." She opened up the partition, and led him to the ramp.

He hesitated, snorting at the scene which greeted him.

"Come on. You'll be fine. Don't take any notice of them.

Just follow me," Jenny whispered. Feeling incredibly calm and positive, she led the way down the ramp, giving him plenty of lead rope so he could pick his way down.

After a slight pause, he followed.

The crowd fell silent.

Jenny caught Dobbin's eye, and couldn't help feeling smug. She led Midnight round the side of the lorry to the waiting boat.

He went tense.

"There's a good boy," she whispered, stroking him.

Captain Dover approached, carrying the canvas sling. Midnight grunted and shied away, nearly knocking Jenny over.

"Can I do that?" Jenny said. "It'll be better if I do it."

But it wasn't any better. In fact, every time she tried to get the sling over his body, Midnight became worse, until he reared right up in the air.

The crowd gasped.

Jenny heard a man say, "This is more like it." She felt like strangling him.

"Please Midnight! Please be a good boy!" she said under her breath. "We've been through so much to get this far. Don't ruin it! Please be good!" In desperation she tried to throw the sling over his back.

Midnight reared again, so high that he nearly fell over backwards, and then plunged forwards, ripping the rope through Jenny's hands.

She hung on valiantly, tears stinging her eyes.

He wheeled round and looked straight at her, trembling.

Frightened, humiliated and dreadfully disappointed, Jenny stared back. Why on earth are you being so *stubborn?* she thought wildly. Why are you being so horrible, after all I've done for you? Don't you see how important this is? You've got to have this sling on! *You've got to!*

"Oh, I can't bear to look! He's scared stiff, the poor thing. If only you'd told me about him, Bob! I'd have given him a home like a shot. He'd have been happy as Larry running with my mares on the moor at Highridge, I know he would. What a pity!"

Jenny couldn't place the voice, but she knew she'd heard it before. Perhaps it was a voice in her head, like a sort of déjà vu. She looked at Midnight, and she didn't see a stubborn, naughty pony any more. She saw a terrified pony re-living the most awful experience of his life, and rapidly losing faith in the one person he thought he could trust. She must have been blind! She'd been so absolutely

determined to make her dream come true that she hadn't noticed it was turning into Midnight's worst nightmare. He'd been screaming at her, and still she hadn't listened.

"Come on, Bob. Let's go. I can't bear to stay a minute longer," Jenny heard the same voice say.

She looked into the crowd, and saw Uncle Bob and his sister, Rose – Jenny remembered her name now – turning to leave.

"No! Wait!" Jenny shouted. "Please don't go! Did you mean it? Did you mean you'd give Midnight a home, running with your mares on the moor?"

Rose pushed through the crowd and came towards her. "Yes, of course I meant it!"

The crowd parted, letting her through. Everyone fell silent, straining to hear the outcome of the drama.

"How much would you want? For livery, I mean? How much will it cost me to keep him with you?" Jenny asked anxiously.

Rose smiled. "Oh, I wouldn't want any money! In fact, if he runs with my mares and gives me some foals, I ought to pay you a stud fee – or we could share the foals, perhaps."

"That sounds fair," said a man standing near Jenny.

"And you'll be welcome to come and see him any time," Rose continued. "It'll be a home for life, free of charge. He'll have acres of moorland to run on with the mares, with some woodland for shelter and a choice of several streams for water. I'll take good care of him, I promise."

By chance, just at the right moment, Midnight pawed at the ground.

"I think that means, yes, please!" Jenny said.

CHAPTER TWENTY-THREE

Mrs Moat, incredibly relieved that disaster had been averted, offered to drive Midnight to Highridge Farm on Bodmin Moor, where Rose and her husband, Harry, lived.

Midnight seemed only too glad to get into the lorry again, away from the boat and the horrible sling.

Captain Dover agreed to postpone sailing until the evening tide. He seemed pretty relieved, too.

Jenny and Ben squashed into the cab of the horse lorry with Mrs Moat. Bob and Rose went on in front, riding in Bob's sports car. Albert went to pick up Ada, so they could join the unexpected party.

The lorry droned and swayed. The cab felt warm. Exhausted, Jenny allowed her eyes to close.

She woke suddenly, slightly embarrassed to find her head resting on Ben's shoulder. "What on earth was that?" she said, sitting up and looking out of the window. "It sounded like thunder!"

Ben laughed. "Don't worry. The lorry's just gone over the cattle grid to Highridge Farm. We've arrived."

Bob, Rose, Harry, Albert and Ada stood waiting for them in the farmyard.

Rose pointed towards a dirt track leading from the yard. "Can you drive up there? It'll be so much easier than leading him all the way, especially if he's a bit excited," she said. "We'll go in front with the Land Rover."

"I'll give it a go," Mrs Moat replied, full of her usual can-do attitude once more.

They drove carefully up the rugged track. The small green fields around the farm rapidly gave way to larger, rougher fields and then open moorland.

It's like a large-scale Lundy, Jenny thought, complete with granite rocks. Midnight will love it! "I'm so glad Bob's your uncle," she said to Ben.

They drove through a gate onto the moorland, and parked on some level ground.

Rose strode away up the hill, and shouted with incredible force, "Hey-up! Hey-up! Come on, girls! Hey-up!" Then she strode back down again.

Midnight whinnied, and pawed the floor of the lorry.

"I think we'd better let him out, before he demolishes my lorry," said Mrs Moat.

Although Jenny's hand stung from the rope burn, she insisted on leading Midnight.

Sweaty and wide-eyed, he skittered down the ramp, but didn't try to pull away.

"Where are the ponies?" Jenny asked anxiously.

"They're coming," Rose said.

Midnight rubbed his sweaty, itchy head against Jenny's arm.

"Don't do that. It hurts,' she said mildly, secretly glad he still liked her. She rubbed his neck.

Suddenly, his head shot up. He whinnied.

A reply came immediately from over the hill.

He squealed, pawed the ground and shook his head with frustration.

Trying to make her painful fingers work properly, Jenny undid the buckle of the headcollar and set him free.

To her surprise, he just stood there, as if trying to take in what had happened. His body quivered with excitement.

A pony came galloping over the hill, then another, and another - seven in all.

Midnight whinnied again, and set off with huge, floating strides towards the herd. He made a bee-line for a strawberry roan. They greeted each other with squeals of joy.

"I'm sure he knows her," Jenny said, thrilled that Midnight had found a friend so quickly.

"I expect so. I bought that mare at Barnstaple Market last autumn, mainly because of her name," Rose said.

"What is it?" Jenny asked.

"Rosie."

"They were best friends on Lundy! Oh, that's brilliant!" Jenny exclaimed.

The mares wheeled and pranced, all trying to impress Midnight. He looked very impressed. In fact, he looked overjoyed.

As the herd cantered down the hill towards her, Jenny realised this was better than her dream. Here Midnight could be wild and free, with his best friend, Rosie, and some other old friends too, by the looks of it. *This* was Midnight's dream.

The ponies came right up to the people gathered by the lorry, skidding and cavorting. One, a pretty mare with amber eyes and a rich golden dun coat, approached Jenny and nuzzled her hand.

Jenny stroked her. "She's beautiful," she said. "Did she come from Lundy, too?"

"Yes," said Rose. "All these mares did, at one time or another. That one's been here several years now, and she's a real sweetheart. Someone on Lundy certainly made an excellent job of taming her. I was given her on condition that she had a good home for life. You arranged it all, didn't you, Albert?" Rose looked at Albert, and then back to Jenny. "Our girls used to ride her a lot when they were here, but now she just runs with the rest of the herd. It's a waste of a good pony, really, and I think she misses all the attention. Perhaps you could take her out sometimes, when you come to visit."

"What's her name?" Jenny asked, knowing in her heart what the answer would be.

"Puffin."

MIDNIGHT

The pony called Midnight in this story is fictional, but based on a real Lundy stallion called Midnight. He was born on the island in the 1930s, and was the dominant stallion from 1945 to 1961. Most of the Lundy ponies alive today are related to him.

Lundy ponies are typically dun-coloured, and Midnight in this story is golden dun. However, the real Midnight was a dark liver chestnut colour, with blonde highlights in his mane and tail and a wide white blaze on his head. He had striking midnight-blue eyes and, by all accounts, was a force to be reckoned with. The lighthouse-keepers called him Boris – after Boris Karloff, the horror film star – because he used to chase them as they walked to the Tavern in the evening.

He was a brilliant jumper. Diana Keast, who used to own Lundy, remembers seeing him jump over walls and slate stiles, roaming where he pleased.

David Dyke, who holidayed on Lundy as a boy, has vivid memories of being cornered by Midnight in the ruins of a cottage, and being rescued by his father, John Dyke.

Midnight hated being handled or stabled. He escaped shipment to the mainland several times by jumping out of the handling pens or, on one occasion, over the shippen wall into Pig's Paradise. In his fascinating book, *My Life on Lundy*, Felix Gade recalls this story and many others, including Midnight's capture.

Eventually Midnight was caught in the autumn of 1961, following a spirited fight which left at least one man injured. He was shipped in the *Lundy Gannet* to the mainland and sold to Mr Chugg, who sold him on at Bampton Fair a few weeks later.

A lady called Peggy Garvey heard from a Romany friend that Midnight was going to Bampton, and she was determined to buy him. Poor Midnight was in a very sad state, and so she managed to buy him for a knock-down price. He had a good home for the remaining five years of his life, running with Peggy's Lundy mares near Okehampton in Devon. He repaid her kindness by siring several lovely foals, which were all good jumpers.

Peggy has many memories of Midnight, like the way he effortlessly cleared five-bar gates from a trot, and the way he used to evade capture by snatching the headcollar out of her hand and running off to drop it at a safe distance before coming back for the edible bribe in a bucket.

However, her most extraordinary memory is of finding Midnight frozen to the spot, barely alive, after a blizzard in the 'Big Freeze' of 1963. She managed to get him back to a warm stable and gently thaw him out. However, as he came round he became dangerously agitated, and Peggy had to hide in a hay rack for several hours until her husband came home from work and rescued her.

Midnight never returned to Lundy,
but his descendants – and his memory – live on.

Other books
by Victoria Eveleigh

Katy's Exmoor
The Story of an Exmoor Pony
ISBN 978 0 9542021 0 1

Katy's Exmoor Adventures
The Sequel to Katy's Exmoor
ISBN 978 0 9542021 1 8

Katy's Exmoor Friends
The Final Part of the Trilogy
ISBN 978 0 9542021 2 5

Tortoise Publishing
West Ilkerton Farm
Devon, EX35 6QA

Telephone (01598) 752310
www.tortoise-publishing.co.uk
sales@tortoise-publishing.co.uk

LUNDY PONIES

Lundy ponies have been bred for about eighty years, but their history could fill a whole book.

The story started in 1928, when Martin Coles Harman brought a herd of forty-one New Forest ponies to Lundy, followed by a Welsh Mountain stallion a couple of years later. One of the stallion's sons, a dun called Pepper, became the herd stallion. During the War, Midnight (Pepper's son) became the dominant stallion. Most of the ponies were sold after the war, leaving about twenty mares with Midnight on the island.

Midnight was sold in 1961, and only ten mares survived the severe winter of 1962-63. Various stallions were used during the next decade, including a Connemara called Rosenharley Peadar and the Lundy stallions Kestrel and Legend of Braetor (both Midnight's sons).

The Harman family sold Lundy to the National Trust in 1969. The National Pony Society (NPS) assumed responsibility for the ponies from 1972 until 1980. On their advice, some of the older mares were put down and most of Rosenharley Peadar's offspring were sold. The NPS registered and branded the Lundy ponies, and used the New Forest stallions Greenwood Minstrel, Midnight Minstrel and Knightwood Grenadier.

During the 1980s, when the NPS was no longer in charge, two Welsh Mountain stallions were used. None of their foals could be registered. Peggy Garvey (who bought Midnight in 1961 and started the Braetor herd) carried on breeding Lundy ponies on the mainland, and the Braetor Lundy Pony Preservation Society was formed. The Society's work proved vital to the survival of the ponies, because by 1990 there were just three registered mares left on Lundy. One of them, Belinda, produced several foals, including a colt called Lundy Sabine (by Braetor Lapwing).

Sabine is the sire of most of the mares on the island today. He now lives near Brayford, with Brian and Jan Symons. They devote a great deal of time to the management of the Lundy ponies. Little Bray Lundy Marisco ('Harry') is the foal in the photo opposite. He's by Lundy Sabine, and out of a New Forest mare called Millersford Starlight. In May 2009, Brian took Starlight and Marisco to Lundy, and a mare called Charlotte Louise (also by Lundy Sabine) was taken to a Connemara stallion on the mainland. It's hoped that this will be the start of a successful new Lundy pony breeding programme.

For information about the Lundy pony sponsorship scheme, please contact Brian and Jan Symons by email Brian.Symons@btinternet.com or telephone (01598) 710294. Further information about Lundy ponies can be found on the Tortoise Publishing website www.tortoise-publishing.co.uk